COWGIRL FALLIN' FOR THE NEIGHBOR

BRIDES OF MILLER RANCH, N.M. BOOK 3

NATALIE DEAN

KENZO PUBLISHING

DEDICATION

I'd like to dedicate this book to YOU! The readers of my books. Without your interest in reading these heartwarming stories of love, I wouldn't have made it this far. So thank you so much for taking the time to read any and hopefully all of my books.

And I can't leave out my wonderful mother, son, sister, and Auntie. I love you all, and thank you for helping me make this happen.

Most of all, I thank God for blessing me on this endeavor.

AND... I've got a special team of advance readers who are always so helpful in pointing out any last minute corrections that need to be made. I'm so thankful to those of you who are so helpful!

EXCLUSIVE BOOKS BY NATALIE DEAN

OTHER BOOKS BY NATALIE DEAN

NATALIE DEAN

BRIDES OF MILLER RANCH, N.M.

MILLER FAMILY SERIES THREE

Cowgirl Fallin' for the Single Dad

Cowgirl Fallin' for the Ranch Hand

Cowgirl Fallin' for the Neighbor

MILLER BROTHERS OF TEXAS (Contemporary)

MILLER FAMILY SERIES TWO

Humbling Her Cowboy

In Debt to the Cowboy

The Cowboy Falls for the Veterinarian

Almost Fired by the Cowboy

Faking a Date with Her Cowboy Boss

BROTHERS OF MILLER RANCH (Contemporary)

MILLER FAMILY SERIES ONE

Her Second Chance Cowboy

Saving Her Cowboy

Her Rival Cowboy

Her Fake-Fiance Cowboy Protector

Taming Her Cowboy Billionaire

BROTHERS OF MILLER RANCH BOX SET

MARRYING A MARSHAL SERIES (Historical)

An Unexpected Treasure

The Dangers of Love

The Outlaw's Daughter

Falling for the Marshal

No Time For Love

MARRYING A MARSHAL BOX SET (includes the above five books, plus the previously unreleased 6th book of my Marrying a Marshal series)

LAWMEN'S BRIDES SERIES (Historical)

The Ranger's Wife

Benjamin's Bride

Carson's Christmas Bride

Justin's Captive Bride

BRIDES AND TWINS SERIES (Historical)

A Soldier's Love

Taming the Rancher

The Wrong Bride

A Surprise Love

The Last Sister's Love

BRIDES & TWINS Box Set / Mail-Order Bride Compilation (My best-seller! It includes TWO MORE unreleased heartwarming mail-order bride series)

LOVE ON THE TRAILS SERIES (Historical)

A Love Beyond Suspicion

Picture Perfect Love

Love of a Wild Rose

A Dangerous Time to Love

A Cold Winter's Love

Brides, Trails, and Mountain Men

Historical Western Romance Compilation

Includes my *Love on the Trails Series* plus an exclusive series titled
Marrying a Mountain Man

BOULDER BRIDES SERIES (Historical)

The Teacher's Bride

The Independent Bride

The Perfect Bride

The Indian's Bride

The Civil War Bride

BOULDER BRIDES BOX SET

BRIDES OF BANNACK SERIES (Historical)

Lottie

Cecilia

Sarah

Though I try to keep this list updated in each book, you may also visit
my website nataliedeanauthor.com for the most up to date
information on my book list.

CONTENTS

Clara

"Man, my waistline isn't going to be happy, but I am so glad you're back!"

Clara smiled flatly at the comment. She knew what her fellow Bible study member meant, but comments like that made her internally roll her eyes.

"I'm glad to be back, to be quite honest! I missed all this too."

She made a gesture to the rest of their Bible study group. It was mostly older folks, but she appreciated them. Often their meetings worked as a time to center herself and do something solely just for her, and having to skip them had worn down on her.

"Oh, my goodness, Clara, this banana nut bread is to *die* for," Marybeth said, approaching her with a small plate with a thick slice of the stuff. "Don't get me wrong, I would be happy if you arrived empty-handed, but I won't lie that I love your baking."

"Thank you. It's my Aunt's recipe."

"Not that I'm complaining, but I'm feeling a little inadequate that you had time to do this on top of everything else you have to do. Does this mean your sister doing better?"

It was no secret amongst anyone in their town how Cass had an awful accident, thanks to an out-of-town driver being tipsy and her trying to drive through a storm. Of course, no one could know that it was going to turn into one of New Mexico's notoriously intense thunderstorms, but driving under the influence was always a risk, bad weather or not.

"She hired someone to pick up on her share of the work, which has been a godsend," Clara said, finishing her own slice of banana nut bread and smiling warmly. The ranch hand, Mick, was new to their operation, but Clara had a wonderful feeling about him. Sure, he was easy on the eyes, but that came second to the fact that he seemed like a decent guy and a hard worker. It was a shame that he would move along too soon, but Clara was familiar with the rhythm of ranch life.

"Oh? That sounds interesting. But I'm glad for it if it frees up time for you."

"You have absolutely no idea."

Marybeth really didn't. Sure, she had a pretty garden in her back yard and raised hunting dogs, but other than that, she was a townie. She didn't know what it was like to rise with the dawn, to take care of chickens, goats and everything else that came from Clara's normal duties, then stacking all of Cass's work on top of that.

It wasn't that Clara wasn't capable of doing all the things

that Cass did; it was just that Cass was so much *better* at them. Somehow, her two older sisters seemed to have been born with the gift of being good with their hands. They could look at things and figure out how they were put together and how they could be taken apart.

Sure, Clara had her own gifts, but those gifts didn't particularly help her with completing her sister's chores.

"I might not, but I do have taste buds, and they're all happy about this whole situation."

Clara chuckled, feeling that warm, fuzzy feeling she got when folks enjoyed her food. There was something just so... *nice* about feeding people and making them feel all satisfied and content.

"I'm sorry, I don't mean to eavesdrop, but did you mention you had more free time lately?"

Clara turned to see Miss Renata standing just to the side, a smile on her kind face. Miss Renata was younger than Papa, but she still had that gravitas that came from an older, respected leader, which was probably why she was the head of many of the church's outreach programs.

"I do! At least before harvest season kicks in. Did you need my help with something?"

Despite how ragged she'd been run lately, Clara felt a sliver of excitement glide through her. She really did miss doing small tasks and helping out at the church. Something about being of service and bringing a smile to someone's face made her feel calmer and more centered. Like she was useful.

She remembered the therapist she'd talked to after her mother passed warning her about basing her worth on how she could help others, but that wasn't what she was doing.

...or at least she was fairly certain she wasn't. Was she?

"Actually, yes! You've always been such a blessing to our meal outreach program, and with Mr. Barker recovering from his carpal tunnel surgery, we're struggling to cover everything. I was hoping you might be willing to do a grocery run and make a few of your delicious, home-cooked meals for one of our farthest out folks."

As always, a compliment to her cooking made Clara grin. Sure, she was teased relentlessly growing up because of her size, because she was quiet, and because she liked plants and animals more than whatever was popular at the time, but as an adult, her cooking made her plenty popular with most of the town.

No one had really apologized to her, outside of Melissa Gainer, Tammy McCree and Jason Hernandez, but those people also didn't get fresh baked cookies, canapes or anything else she put her heart into.

Their loss.

"Oh, I'd love to! When do you need me to head out?"

"Honestly, if you could visit him tomorrow, that would be amazing."

"I can do that. Can you email me his allergies and address?" That was another great thing about the outreach program; Clara had never been very good at organization, but Miss Renata had a whole database of who needed what help, their preferences and any dietary restrictions. After all, Clara wouldn't buy the same groceries for a diabetic as she would for someone recovering from heart surgery.

"I'll do that right now. I was actually heading to my office as we speak. Thank you again, Clara. It's *so* good to have you back." The older woman passed by her, patting Clara's arm as she went. "You help us so much more than you know."

Clara beamed; her mood bolstered even further. It was a

little thing, sure, but it was further proof that she could make a difference in people's lives. Further proof that she mattered.

She missed that feeling, that was for sure, and although she loved Cass dearly, she was so glad she was going to be able to get back involved with the town again.

2

Nathan

*H*uh, *has that stain always been there?*

Nate laid there on the cool linoleum; his gaze stuck on a grayish patch just under part of his counter. His breath was wheezing out of his lungs, sounding more like ghosts of the condemned rather than actual inhalation. He hated that sound, and yet it was impossible to ignore. Maybe because his chest ached every time it happened, like it was trying to expand but something was holding it in place.

Of course, it's always been there. It's not like I've been able to cook in here for months.

Nathan groaned and attempted to roll on his side, but he only managed a bit of a jerk before nausea swept through him with a vengeance. Who'd have thought a side-effect of being struck by lightning was vertigo.

"Right, stay still. Got it."

He wanted to get up, he did. He wanted to grab that glass of water he'd left up on the counter so high above him and quench the thirst that was still plaguing him. Some of his meds gave him the *worst* dry mouth.

It wasn't a great feeling, naturally, and it made him uncomfortable. And being uncomfortable made him angry. It was just dry mouth, and yet he was nearly incapacitated from it.

Breathe. Just concentrate on your breathing, and it'll pass.

He preferred to talk to himself when such fits overtook him, but he didn't have the breath for it. At least not yet. He was just going to need to be still, be calm, and let his body settle down.

...easier said than done.

The floor wasn't exactly comfortable, even if the cool surface felt nice against his heated skin, and he could feel his back and tailbone starting to ache. There had been a time where he'd been muscular with a little extra padding that came from being real good at providing for himself, but that time had long since passed, leaving him thin, wiry and a bit gaunt.

Nathan *hated* that.

He'd never thought of himself as particularly vain but seeing his hard-won muscles disappear had been a blow.

One would think the fact that he sat so much would have given him a little more padding, but apparently not. His body had metabolized almost all of his muscle, and he just didn't have enough motivation to cook enough to meet his calorie intake for the day.

Besides, considering that even getting water had him wheezing on the floor, it probably wasn't a good idea to use the oven.

Thirst prickled at him again, even more vicious. Time to try again.

"Here we go," Nate whispered, summoning all his energy

and trying to get at least his arm up to grab the edge of the counter and pull himself up.

He reached. He reached and *reached*, but his fingers slipped right off the edge of the counter and his arm smacked to the ground, sending more vertigo rushing through his mind. What a mess.

His wheelchair was still too far out of his reach, his body was refusing to sit up, and he was *thirsty*.

"You've gotta be kidding me," he growled to himself.

But no, it wasn't a joke. It was his awful, awful reality that had been awful for so long he'd forgotten what it was like for things to *not* be awful.

He'd just been getting water. That was it. Just a quick trip to his kitchen and he'd gotten winded like some sort of asthmatic. He'd stopped, of course, leaned over the counter and tried to catch his breath, but then the dizziness swept in with a vengeance.

Thankfully, he'd learned something during his time in recovery, and he quickly got down on the ground to splay himself across the cool floor. It wasn't the most dignified thing, but it was better than trying to fight it and then falling. He'd done that once, back in the early days, only to clip his head on the corner of his bathroom sink and end up splitting some of his scar tissue in a tearing wound.

Now *that* had certainly been a lesson.

But even though he had done the right thing, health-wise, anger still rolled through him, hot and stabbing. He was chock full of it, full to bursting until all that hate-runoff spilled out of his soul and across the floor. Faintly, Nate wondered if his whole house was stained in the feeling, the bitter rage seeping into the floorboards and painting the walls.

He shouldn't have refused that home health aide. He knew

that. But he was a grown man, and the thought of some hired worker from the city coming into his home and taking care of him like a baby made his pride burn white-hot.

"I used to be so capable," he hissed to himself, like stating that would change anything. But it was true. He'd been a homesteader in the very farthest reaches of the area, and he'd only gone into town maybe twice a month for the occasional church service or night at the bar. He fished. He trapped. He raised and grew his food. He preserved, harvested and lived off the land almost entirely. Sure, he'd buy occasional things from the town grocery, but mostly, it was just him and what the earth gave him.

But now?

He's nothing. Not a homesteader. Not a farmer. Just a scarred invalid who couldn't even get himself some water. He was...

He was just so *tired*. Too exhausted to get up and into his chair and too angry to just nap where he was and recuperate. It wouldn't be the first time he'd fallen asleep on the floor. Why did everything have to be just so hard and impossible these days?

Those feelings rose up in him, making the dizziness worse, making his breaths wheeze more. He was caught up in a maelstrom that he knew was unhealthy, but it wasn't like he could do anything about it. There was no escaping, no—

Just when it seemed like it was going to reach its peak, a solid knock sounded on his door.

Who on earth could that be?

3
_____

Clara

$\mathcal{C}$lara finished placing the butter in the bottom of her roast pan and went about adding the seasoning. So many people forgot that step, leaving their food flavorful on the top but lacking on the bottom. An especially tragic loss, considering that the melted fat that naturally dripped downward and collected in the bottom of the pan would then distribute the seasoning all over the vegetables that she would add later.

Goodness, Clara loved cooking. The ins and outs of it, the secret little tricks of it and the science of how things blended together. It was wonderful, really, and she never tired of it.

"Oooh, whatcha up to in here?" Charlie asked, coming up behind her and kissing the top of her head. As her only sibling that was taller than her, he was the only one who could do that, and Clara got the feeling he reveled in that fact. Little brothers sure were strange sometimes.

"Just making a roast for the church's meal outreach program."

"Wow, you're back on that? I thought everything with Cass was taking up your time?"

"Well, it was, but that Mick gentleman really has practically gotten things back to normal."

"Yeah, he seems alright." Charlie narrowed his eyes as he looked out the window. "I always get nervous whenever we take on a temp worker, but so far it's been good."

"Why is that, Charlie?"

She tried to phrase it lightly, casually, but she wasn't quite sure she succeeded. Charlie was an outgoing, extroverted type growing up, but since he'd come back after dropping out of college, he'd been much more of a homebody.

Sure, he still went out, still visited his friends in town and in the city, but there was a... a sort of caution he didn't have before.

Strange.

"I know you've got everybody else fooled, but don't think I can't tell when you're trying to psychoanalyze me."

"I'm not trying to psychoanalyze—"

"Yeah, yeah, you keep telling yourself that. But to answer, I just have a hard time even wanting to get to know and trust someone when I know that they're just gonna move on in three months. There's nothing wrong with being a nomadic type of person, but, I dunno. Just not for me, I guess. I want to get to know someone inside and out if they're gonna be around my home."

Clara hadn't been expecting such an honest answer, and she stopped her seasoning to look her brother over. "Are you upset we hired him?"

"What? No, not at all. In fact, I was the one who suggested

Cass hire someone. I'm glad he's here. I'm just, uh, background worried, I guess."

"It was your idea?"

Charlie nodded, coming around the island to lean against the counter. "Yeah. Remember when she had that fall after playing frisbee out with Savannah? Well, I got real with her, told her what was what, and that she needed to stop lying to Charity."

"...and that worked?"

Clara didn't mean to sound so surprised, but their second-eldest sister was known for her determination as well as her stubborn streak. She was a proud woman who took her work on the ranch very seriously, second only to Charity.

"Believe it or not, it did. I don't think I said anything Cass didn't already know. Sometimes, you just gotta hear someone confirm what you're thinking before you're ready to admit it to yourself."

"I suppose so." Clara reached up with salty fingers and pinched his cheek. He was far too old for the gesture, but that was exactly why she did it. "Look at you, psychoanalyzing with the best of 'em."

"Hey, hey, *hey,* watch the face!"

He pulled away from her and attempted to ruffle her hair, but she dodged and brandished her meat fork at him. "You better stop if you know what's good for you," she warned, trying not to laugh.

Both of Charlie's hands went up and he gave her a skeptical sort of look. "Oh, so we're threatening people now?"

"It seems we are," she managed to answer before they both broke into laughter.

Goodness, it had been so *long* since they'd been goofy together. So needlessly silly.

Ever since Cass's accident, there had been a solemn sort of silence over the house. Especially when they hadn't even known if she would survive. Clara tried not to think of that night, or the days following it, but their weight had blanketed the house in a tangible sort of dread.

And then, when Cass had first come home, it hadn't gotten much better. She was either in pain, unconscious, or snapping at someone. It was like she wasn't even herself anymore, and although Clara told herself to be as patient as possible, she couldn't lie that she missed the way her sister used to be.

Granted, she had the feeling that Cass missed the old her even more.

Calming herself, Clara let out a wistful sort of hum and got back to cooking. To her surprise, Charlie stayed with her, doing whatever small task she asked him to do until everything was safely tucked into the oven.

"That's got a while to cook, if I remember, right?"

Clara nodded. "Low and slow for five to six hours."

"Phew. I don't know how you have the patience. Especially since this starts to smell heavenly after about half an hour."

"You really want to know my secret?" Clara asked, keeping her tone level as if she were serious. It was a trick she'd learned long ago, and even after her twenty-eight years on earth, her siblings almost always fell for it. Maybe it was just because she was usually a fairly genuine person. Certainly not a bad thing, in her opinion.

"You bet, I wanna know."

Clara leaned in close, like she was going to tell her little brother a secret. "You just go and clean out the bedding in the chicken coop. Takes a while, and then after that you'll definitely need to take a shower. Feel free to thank me later. By then, several hours will have gone by."

He made a scoffing sound and tried to ruffle her hair again, just for him to slap his hand against her spatula.

"You're hilarious. You know, if you want me to do one of your chores for you, you could just ask. Or, you know, hire an independent contractor."

"I think one of those at a time is plenty for now," Clara said with a laugh.

"Fair point. A lot of changes around here the past few years, some of them good. A lot bad."

Clara thought of Cass and nodded. "Yeah. A lot bad."

"But at least Charity's got Alejandro. And Savannah sure does bring plenty of life here."

Clara couldn't deny that. Not that she even wanted to. Savannah brought an energy to their ranch that hadn't been around in at least six or seven years, one that came with youth and the excitement of discovering everything for the first time.

It was too bad that there weren't more little ones to run about. But Charity was still very early in her relationship with Alejandro. And Cass was so injured that she could find the perfect partner tomorrow and there still wouldn't be any chance of a little one from her. And as for Clara herself... well...

There weren't exactly a lot of options out there for her.

It wasn't that their town was full of hateful people, per se, but there was a noted lack of bachelors. Actually, of eligible single people in general. It seemed practically everyone in town was matched up with someone, leaving precious few to date.

And it didn't help that Clara was... picky.

It wasn't that she thought she was better than other people, not at all. It was just most of her worst bullies growing up were the prettiest and most popular at school, giving her a sort of aversion to people most others found attractive. On top of that, she wasn't really interested in going out, or drinking, or anything that she knew people thought rich people were into.

Clara just wanted to wear pretty dresses, have nice makeup, and take care of her animals while someone held her hand.

Was that too much to ask for? Apparently so.

"Hey, what's with that glum look on your face?" Charlie asked, bringing her back to the present.

"Huh? Nothing, sorry. I was just thinking about how long I should set my timer. Do you want to go with me to help with the chicken coop?"

"Well, if I'm being honest, I don't think I could ever really *want* that, but I don't mind helping you out."

"Brat," she accused with a laugh.

"Yeah, but that's part of my charm."

"You keep telling yourself that."

"I will. And I'll tell you too. Maybe if I do it enough times, you'll believe me."

"I wouldn't hold your breath," she quipped, setting a timer on her phone and heading out the door, Charlie right behind her.

"I dunno. If we're cleaning the bedding in the coop, maybe holding my breath would be a good thing."

"Har, har, you're hilarious."

He gave her a cheeky look, and then the two of them were out the door and heading towards the coop.

CLARA FOLLOWED the uneven dirt path, her Jeep bouncing along smoothly. She knew that Nathan was out in the boonies and that her GPS was next to useless to get her there, so she was going off the directions Miss Renata had emailed her. He was about twice the distance from town as her own ranch, and she liked the quiet of it.

It took her about twenty minutes to pull up to the front, but she wasn't worried about the roast getting cold. She'd made sure to cook it in one of her special containers that was meant to retain food and keep it piping hot for over two hours of travel time. She couldn't imagine showing up just to deliver cold food in some congealed drippings. Gross.

"Cute place," she commented to herself, looking it over.

It was a quaint sort of cabin, big enough not to be cramped but clearly small enough that she knew every space in it was probably utilized to its fullest potential. There was a large garden up front, not quite as impressive as Papa's but large nonetheless. What was clearly a potato and squash patch was next to it, and then further beyond that was a chicken coop.

"Aww, I wonder who's all roosted in there?" Clara said as she got out, circling around to pull the heavy roast tray out from where it was cushioned on a blanket in her front seat.

There was a pigpen to the left of the house, well enough away that the smell probably didn't carry inside too often. She could see a water pump and she bet he had some sort of drip irrigation in his garden.

All in all, it was a nice little homestead. Sure, he didn't have goats, horses or cattle, nor large grazing pens, but she could see it being enough to meet almost all of his needs.

And also, a whole lot of work.

Heading up to his front door, she set her roast to the side and gave a solid knock. Given what she knew about the man she was helping, it might take him a couple of minutes to greet her. But after a few solid minutes, she couldn't help but feel like too much time was passing.

Clara liked to think that she was a patient person, but with everything that had happened with Cass, she couldn't help the prickle of apprehension that went up the back of her neck. Normally, whenever her recovering sister was taking too long for something, it almost always meant she fell or was otherwise in trouble.

"Hello? Mr. Westbrook?" she called.

There was no answer. Her apprehension grew. Moving to the side, she peered into the small front window, her blood running cold when she saw a slippered foot on the kitchen floor.

That definitely looked like he fell.

"Mr. Westbrook! I'm coming in!"

Clara returned to the front door, taking a deep breath and centering herself. She'd read when she was younger that the best way to break down a door was to kick it just under the handle, so she figured that was exactly what she was going to do.

Probably not the best day to wear a pair of cute wedges.

At least they were low ones, not even two inches. She could take them off, but she wasn't particularly keen on kicking the door with all her might while her feet were bare.

"Come on, Clara, one, two, three!"

With all the force she could muster, she brought her knee out then kicked outwards just like Papa had taught her. The sole of her shoe slammed into her target, and suddenly the door burst open with a pop.

She was definitely going to need to fix that later.

But the door didn't matter for the moment. She rushed forward, roast container forgotten outside. Sure enough, there the man was, sprawled out on his kitchen floor, breathing harshly.

Thank goodness for those ragged breaths, because otherwise she might have thought him dead. Instead, she swallowed hard, realizing that she had just broken into the man's house and that he was glaring bloody murder at her.

"Who the heck are you!?"

4

Nathan

Out of nowhere, there was a giant woman in his house.

Nathan blinked at her, wondering if he had passed out and was suddenly hallucinating. Unlikely, but so was being struck by lightning—and that had already happened to him.

She had to be over six feet tall and was dressed in some sort of dress out of the fifties, with her hair done up in intricate-looking curls. That couldn't be real. No one dressed like that anymore.

"Apologies for my sudden entrance. My name's Clara. I —_Oh!_ I'll be right back!"

And just like that, she marched out, returning moments later with a fancy looking tray with an even fancier looking cover.

"I was sent here as part of the church's outreach program that you signed up for. I brought you dinner and have some groceries in the car. I do apologize for bursting in, but when I saw you on the floor, well... I suppose you can say it struck a chord. Can I help you up or are you purposefully there?"

"Why would I be purposefully on the floor?" Nathan heard himself snap. He was still caught up in the shock of it all. It wasn't every day that a stranger barreled into his house. Hadn't he locked the door?

"It's not my place to worry about that, is it? Perhaps it's cooler down there. Sometimes, my brother likes to stretch out and pop his back on the ground."

That... wasn't the response he had been expecting. At least she wasn't patronizing him. He *hated* being patronized. Just because he was an invalid didn't mean he didn't have any dignity.

"But you didn't quite answer the question. Would you like some help up?"

"I'm—no. I don't need any help." He felt his cheeks coloring, embarrassed that he was caught in such a compromising state. A grown man trapped on the floor just because he was too weak to right himself.

"Alright then. Would you like a glass of water?"

He narrowed his eyes at her, wondering if she was mocking him, but she seemed earnest enough. Despite her strange getup, she didn't seem to be making a production of anything, just walking around his kitchen matter-of-factly.

Besides, that intense thirst he'd been nursing reasserted itself, his tongue still sandpapered and thick.

"...yeah."

"Okay then. I'll get that for you."

His pride stung that he had to accept her help, but he waited patiently as she rummaged through his cupboard for a glass then crossed to her fridge. Her maroon heels that she clicked around him certainly made it a lot easier to track her movements.

"Um, where's your water pitcher?"

"I don't have one," he answered flatly.

He expected some sort of comment about that, or how tap water was unhealthy, but instead the fridge door just shut, and she walked over to his sink. Water ran, and the next thing he knew, she was handing him a glass of water.

It was as he reached out for it that the silliness of the situation truly hit him. Some rockabilly dressed tall woman was walking around his kitchen in her pretty, shiny heels, while he was laid out on the floor of his own kitchen. The sheer strangeness of it motivated him to sit up, and he struggled to do so.

It wasn't easy. Not at all. His back screamed at him and his muscles just shook and shook. He felt like he was being pulled thin, stretched into taffy. He tried, he really did, but his body just wouldn't cooperate.

Rage bubbled up in him again, its absence incredibly short, and he felt it bubble out of his mouth.

"Are you enjoying watching me suffer?" he hissed, poison flowing from every syllable.

"Hmm, I apologize. I was just finding a place for the roast to rest since you said you didn't need help. But I'm happy to do so if you'd give me permission."

Permission? Who even talked like that? He didn't know, but he found himself irritated at admitting he did.

"Yeah, I guess."

"Alright then."

As calm as anything, she undid the brakes of his wheelchair, pushing it closer before reapplying them again. Then she crouched beside him, angling herself so that her skirts still covered her, and just like that, she was pulling him to his feet with ease.

While Nathan had lost plenty of weight, he still wasn't *light* by any means, and he found himself staring at her in shock as she maneuvered him over to his chair. Just how strong was this giant woman?

"Here, let me get that water for you," she said once he was settled, grabbing it from the floor and handing it to him once again. "Let me know if you want more."

She wore such a sweet smile; her plump lips painted a deep maroon to match her shoes. She was very put together, he noticed as the shock of her bursting into his house began to wear off. Like something out of a magazine from the 1940s. A relic from a bygone era.

But her polish, her poise, only made him angrier and more embarrassed. He wanted to be a good host to her, to prove that he didn't need charity from a stranger. But he also wanted her to just leave and let him rot right where he was. But before he could go in either direction, a flurry of *very* angry clucks and shrieks sounded from outside.

"Goodness, some cluckers are having a very serious conversation, aren't they?" the Clara woman asked with that same warm smile.

"Yeah, they do that from time to time."

"I'm well aware," she said, practically lighting up. "Can I go give them a visit?"

But it was only bitterness that poured from his mouth. "Sure, and while you're there, why don't you just feed them and harvest the eggs I couldn't get to?"

He meant it as sarcastic. *Anyone* could tell that he was being sarcastic, and yet, she just kept on smiling.

"Sure. I can do that."

And then she was out the door before he could even formulate a response.

...what on earth was going on?

He sat there a few moments, sure that it was a prank, but when he rolled to the window, he saw her clomping towards his chicken coop.

Huh.

Stranger things had happened, he supposed, but he still didn't know what to think about that.

It felt creepy to keep watching her, however, so he instead refilled his water glass and went to use the restroom. He felt unsettled, like his scarred skin was too small for his body, and that feeling didn't abate until she came in a little over half an hour later.

She had her shoes in one hand, a large basket that he didn't recognize in the other and was still grinning broadly. With a tip of her head, she walked past him and set the basket in his kitchen a bit away from the roast.

"I ended up with quite a few eggs, and I changed the bedding while I was in there. You should be good for a little bit. You have a good night, Mr. Westbrook."

Another nod and then she was walking out again. Nathan watched her, wondering if he'd ended up in an episode of the Twilight Zone, only for her to pause at the door and shoot him a soft look over her shoulder.

Why was she looking at him like that? Was she pitying him?

"The roast tastes best hot, so please enjoy it as soon as you're ready. I already set the rest of the groceries in your fridge."

She did? When?

But he didn't ask that, and she didn't answer, instead heading out to the Jeep that she'd arrived in. She drove away without a look back, her hair somehow staying in place even with the windows all the way down.

That... that was weird, right? People didn't just barge into other people's houses and bring them food, then clean their chicken coops. Besides, they lived in a small town, one where he knew most faces, and everyone definitely knew his because of the nature of his accident. Clara... Clara... that named seemed so familiar. Maybe she worked at their local grocery shop?

The answer kept eluding him, so Nathan gave up. He could feel exhaustion wearing at him, so food would definitely do him some good. Wheeling into the kitchen, he lifted the lid of the fancy container and saw a truly glorious, massive roast surrounded by a plethora of delicious-smelling vegetables. It was like something out of a movie, so large and perfectly caramelized that he knew it had to cost quite a pretty penny.

And that *smell.* It was perfect. Wonderful. Rich and aromatic with a hint of citrus underneath.

Then it hit him, right after the heady scent practically had him floating. Only one family in the town could spend so much money on a sizable roast and not even bat an eye.

That giant woman was a Miller.

5

Clara

Clara opened the door, standing outside on the porch and leaning in just far enough so she could shout inside.

"Hey, can anyone get me a damp cloth? And, uh, maybe some sani-wipes?"

Sure, she could just text, but her phone was tucked into the pocket she'd sewn into her dress and she didn't feel like fishing it out.

"I've got you," Papa's voice came from upstairs, drifting down to her over the banister. Clara waited patiently, and soon enough, her father was indeed striding towards her with both items in hand.

"No offense, my dear, but you look a right mess. Weren't you just delivering a dinner?"

"I was, but I got wrapped up in some chores. Messy chores, of course."

"And so you just decided that you needed to do them barefoot?"

"Well, I wasn't about to get chicken matter all over these cute wedges."

Papa chuckled, leaving her for a moment then returning with the small trashcan from their downstairs bathroom. Clara gratefully deposited her used sanitation wipes into them, trying to make sure she got most of the gross stuff off.

"Trust my little fashionista to make sure she saved her shoes."

"You better believe it," she answered with a grin.

Sure, at first Papa had had no idea what to do with his daughter who loved makeup, fashion and classic movies, but over the years he'd seem to have gotten the gist of most of it. He wasn't about to watch any fashion shows or know the difference between four-way-stretch spandex or quality cotton, but he didn't mock her and encouraged her hobby. He was always so good that way.

"Here, let me get you another cloth. I have a feeling you're going to need it."

"You're a godsend," Clara breathed happily.

He gave her that knowing Papa grin, then did just as he said. After that, it took her maybe ten more minutes to get herself as wiped down as she wanted, and while she was doing that, she explained everything that had happened at Nathan's house.

"It was just so sad, you know? He has this neat, well-put-together little operation that he probably had no problem running before. But now, with... you know, everything that he has to go through, he's clearly struggling."

"Hits a little close to home, doesn't it?" Papa asked, setting the trashcan back in the bathroom while Clara finally was able to step into her home.

"It does. I couldn't help but compare it to so much of what Cass has gone through, or what we've gone through with her. And we're a family; he has *no one*, it seems."

"You're right. That is sad. I wouldn't be here now if it weren't for you and your siblings."

That made her heart ping in an entirely different way. "Exactly. Just doesn't feel right."

"You've always had a very open, loving heart, Clara. I'm not surprised that you would pick up on his frustration." Papa stopped for a moment, giving her a discerning look. "Did you remember to eat before you went off to save the day?"

Clara grinned sheepishly. "No, I was too excited."

"Right. Well, you go change yourself and wash, n' I'll make you a grilled sammie."

"Ah, *bless* you," Clara said, crossing to him and pressing a kiss to his cheek.

"It's what I'm here for."

Clara hurried upstairs, eager to wash and put on more casual in-house clothes. It wasn't that she was overly grossed out by cleaning chicken mess—she was in charge of their coop at home, after all. It was just that she liked to have her farming clothes for farming things while her nice clothes were more for going out. Crossing the two and doing an animal chore in her specially made retro dress just felt entirely *wrong*.

Thankfully, it wasn't that hard to wash the feeling away with copious amounts of hot water. Soon she was indeed perched on a stool in the kitchen, drinking some hibiscus and elderberry tea while Papa finished up the sandwich he was grilling.

It smelled like heaven, as Papa's cooking usually did. Although he'd never really shared her love of fashion and style, they had always shared their passion for cooking, and seeing him at the oven never failed to make her feel so at home.

"Sammie's up," he said with a grin, sliding a plate to her.

"Thanks, Papa."

"Of course."

A few moments later, he sat down across from her with a sandwich of his own. They ate and talked about their day, and the three-pound tomato that one of their tomato plants had produced, when Papa suddenly cleared his throat.

"You alright there?" Clara asked with a chuckle.

"Yes. Actually, I just had an idea."

"Oh, about what?"

"This fellow's situation. Why don't you pull a Mick and just help him?"

Clara blinked at her father. "You want me to get him to hire me as a farm hand?"

"Well, not the money part, but the rest of it. Consider it donating your time and effort. Can't imagine it going to a better cause considering all he's gone through."

At that, Clara felt a bubbling grin spread across her features, impossible to resist. "That, Papa, might be the best idea I've ever heard."

"Whoa. Well, I don't know about that considering how bright you lot are, but I'll take the compliment nonetheless."

"You better. I'm persistent."

"If there's anything that's true, it's that."

They shared a little more conversation and a few laughs as they finished up their sandwiches. After placing their dishes in the washer, Clara went upstairs and started to put together a new sort of schedule that would help her get her own chores done as well as Nathan's. It wouldn't be easy, that was for certain, but she was sure Charlie and even Mick could cover a chore or two once a week without much problem.

Suddenly, it was a whole lot more convenient that Clara was the early bird of her family. Happily humming to herself, she pulled up her calendar program that she usually used for seedling planning and got to work.

6

Nathan

Nathan looked down at his Giant Mountain leek seeds and his American Flag leeks, wondering which one he should plant. Normally his rampant love of leek soup would have him indulging with both varieties. But considering how little of his garden he'd gotten amended so far, it wasn't likely he'd be able to handle both.

Or be able to handle most of his squash. Or his corn. In fact, his entire fall garden was probably going to be halved.

…if he was lucky to be able to handle even that much.

"Ugh, you gotta be kidding me," Nathan snapped, flopping back in his chair. But before any curses could tumble past his lips, a semi-familiar Jeep pulled up.

It was *her.*

Again.

The giant lady stepped out, but unlike when they first met,

she was dressed much more practically in overalls and a tank top.

Huh, had she come back for her fancy container? It'd only been a day. It wasn't like he could eat that much delicious roast in a single day. Although he certainly had tried. That meat had been so tender and melt-in-his-mouth that he'd practically cried.

Not that he would ever admit that.

"Hey there, I brought some more groceries. You want me to put them in the kitchen for you to organize later or just shove them into the fridge?"

Nathan just stared at her, wondering if her bizarre behavior was just a rich people thing or if all of the Millers were a little... weird.

"Just put whatever in the fridge," he answered tersely. Suddenly he didn't want to be anywhere near the woman. Somehow, she was even more intimidating without her heels, her broad frame in a much more solid stance. "I'm gonna... go haul some food over to the pigs."

"Right. Sounds like a plan," she said, as cheery as anything. Despite her more practical, durable outfit, her lips were painted a pretty, pretty pink, making her cheeks seem to glow with that color too. But her being put together just made Nathan feel that much worse, with his scars and marred skin and... well, *everything.*

Why don't you just kick her out? he asked himself as he went about grabbing the food and a pail, then hauling them in his lap as close as he could get to the pigpen. He couldn't get quite all the way up to the fence with his chair, considering how uneven and muddy the ground was, unfortunately, so the last bit required him to stand and complete the chore.

Praying that his legs didn't give way, Nathan went about it as best he could, but he was barely halfway through with it when he had to stop and rest in his chair.

How miserable.

Flopping back in his chair for a breather, Nathan realized in his entire struggle to feed his livestock, he never noticed the woman leave. Was... was she still around?

No, that seemed incredibly unlikely. She was rich and had a ranch of her own; most likely she dropped off the food and boogied away from his slum of a place as soon as she could. People like her loved doing charity work, or the easy stuff that involved throwing their copious amounts of money at things. They didn't actually want to be uncomfortable or do real work.

But... try as he might to convince himself of that, a niggling feeling in the back of his mind had him eventually rolling back into his house. He told himself he was just being cautious—she could be stealing something after all!

Then again, wasn't her family filthy rich? What could she possibly want that he had?

The answer came when he found her still in the kitchen, elbow-deep in suds and dishwater with an apron tied in a pretty bow behind her back. Where it had come from, he didn't know. Similarly, he had no idea where she'd procured the yellow gloves she was wearing as she dutifully scrubbed along, humming to herself like she was doing something pleasant instead of scraping month old oatmeal paste out of a dirty bowl.

What on earth...

Nathan could only stare, completely incredulous. Washing his gross, neglected dishes by hand definitely didn't fit into easy work.

Some part of Nate knew that he should say something, should clear his throat or otherwise announce his presence, but he was dumbfounded. The sight was strangely domestic, considering the woman was practically a total stranger, and yet entirely bizarre at the same time.

It was Clara who, in the end, turned and noticed him, letting out a short, sharp cry and jumping.

"Goodness gracious, friend, you gave me a start there! I really was in my own little world, wasn't I?"

The smile she flashed him was dazzling and sweet, but that only rubbed against him more. For every pretty thing that the woman did, it just made him feel grosser and more helpless, like some sort of cretin at her feet.

It hadn't always been that way. Before being struck by lightning, Nate had known he was at least somewhat pleasant looking. No Hollywood heartthrob, of course, but he got by well enough. Sure, he hadn't dated since moving to town and starting up his homestead, but that was largely because he was so busy.

And that bachelor life suited him. He liked having his own schedule and being accountable to no one else but his animals. He liked going into town for a drink if he wanted or watching an entire trilogy of movies in the living room in nothing but his ratty boxers.

Too bad all of that had gone out the window when God had decided he deserved to be struck by lightning.

"Are you alright there? Do you need a glass of water?"

"Huh?" Ugh, her pleasant, lovely tone grated against his ears. He just wanted to be alone to rot in his misery! Why was she so... so... so bright and cheery? "No. I'm fine."

"Good to hear." She turned off the tap and turned fully to him, somehow beaming even brighter. That didn't seem physically possible, as humans only had so many teeth, and yet... "Is there anything else I can help you with once these dishes are done?"

Wait... what? She wanted to *keep* going?

7

Clara

Clara had meant to ask permission or at least explain herself before she started doing things, but the moment she'd finished putting away the groceries, the dishes started calling to her. The next thing she knew, she was elbow-deep in suds.

It probably wasn't the politest way to go about it, but she could tell from the pile-up that Nathan likely didn't have the extra energy to get such a tedious chore done, especially since he would have to stand at the sink instead of sitting in his chair. And, although his injuries were clearly nothing like her sister's, she'd learned from watching Cass's recovery just how exhausting standing for any length of time could be.

So when she'd turned around and nearly jumped out of her skin, she wasn't surprised to see that Nathan was irritated with her; she was being rather presumptuous. She just hoped the idea of having clean dishes again was enough to temper any frustration he had with her.

Goodness, he really did remind her of Cass in several ways. But she didn't know if either of them would be flattered by such a comparison.

"What do you mean?"

Ouch. His tone was sharp and biting, but Clara let it flow off her. Again, she knew from her experiences with Cass how to deal with a sourpuss whose pride was hurting from their body not doing what they wanted it to. Sweetness and charity would only make the situation worse, especially if he thought she pitied him at all. No, it was time to be forthright, direct and maybe even a bit blunt.

"Look, ever since our new guy started, he's been knocking it out of the park, and I find myself with so much extra time that I'm actually getting bored. I noticed you had some stuff to do around here, so I figured I might as well occupy myself until my sister gets home from her physical therapy."

There, state it like she was spoiled, and he was doing *her* a solid. Clara tried not to hold her breath or look hopeful, but it was difficult given her nature.

"Are you kidding me?" he asked, his voice low but layered with shock. Yikes, definitely not the tone she was hoping for.

"Hold that thought. I'm going to take out the trash."

Clara was certainly aware that he was staring at her with an open mouth, but she promptly ignored that. Hopefully giving him a couple minutes of space would allow him to really think about her idea instead of having a knee-jerk reaction against it.

And hey, if she also managed to do some other chores while she was outside... well, that was just a happy coincidence, wasn't it?

"It's not like he's going to stop me in the middle of it."

Or at least she hoped not.

...maybe it would do her well to actually ask him. But what if he said no? She supposed that was his right, but it hurt her heart that he was clearly overwhelmed by everything around him.

Compromise. She didn't go all the way inside but instead stood at the base of his porch and called out to him. "Hey, do you want me to finish up feeding the pigs?"

There wasn't an answer for a long, long moment, and Clara was about to head in to ask again when Nathan finally answered.

"Yeah, might as well since you're out there."

There! She had permission. Sure, maybe she didn't get it in the most up-front way, but the important thing was *he* was the one doing *her* a favor.

"Alright, thanks. I could use the workout."

He didn't reply, but that was okay. He didn't need to.

Whistling to herself, Clara headed over to the pigpen. He really hadn't done all that bad on his own, but she couldn't blame him for getting exhausted. The bag of feed was fairly new, so still plenty heavy. Maybe the next time she popped by, she would bring some sort of very big ladle or a feeder scoop. She was sure they had at least one spare one laying around.

Mission set, she felt a lot better. Even if he kicked her out, she'd gotten two major chores done and supplied him with at least enough food to last a couple weeks. Sure, she hoped he would let her linger around—especially with the fall planting season rolling in—but she wasn't going to count her chickens before they were hatched.

...speaking of chickens...

"No, Clara, keep your head on straight. Pigs today. Maybe chickens tomorrow."

Then again, it wouldn't hurt anything if she made sure they'd gotten enough feed since the day before.

"Hah, you just can't help yourself, can you?" she murmured. When she was younger, her siblings used to tease how often she talked to herself, but over the years they'd gotten just as used to it as she was. Especially since she tended to do it the most when she was sewing.

And sure, maybe homesteading chores weren't quite the same as sewing herself up a pretty dress, but they were adjacent... sort of. Maybe.

"Hello there, you gorgeous ladies. You ready for some more grub?"

The sows all grunted in agreement while their male counterparts on the other half of the pen whined for attention in typical boar fashion.

"Don't worry, you lot. I'll be right with you. Ladies first, after all."

The chorus of piggy arguments that arose from them was borderline hysterical, and Clara couldn't help but laugh. Animals were so funny, and she wasn't surprised that Nathan's little herd had plenty of personality. What she was surprised by was that they hadn't tried to destroy their pen or the double barrier between the males and females. Pigs were incredibly intelligent and could get stressed out if they thought their owner was sick or hurt, or if they felt neglected by their human. They really had to trust Mr. Westbrook to be so well behaved even when he couldn't spend nearly as much time with them.

And that fact made her heart warm. She was glad that she was helping someone who had so obviously poured so much love into his homestead and animals. It wasn't fair, what had happened to him, just like it wasn't fair what happened to Cass, and maybe, just maybe, Clara could help balance the scales a bit.

It didn't take her long to finish up, and she also took the time to pick up some of the clutter in his front yard and sweep his porch. But when she was finished, she couldn't really think of anything to do without his permission, and she was still reluctant to go back inside.

"I suppose it's time to face the dragon," she muttered to herself, standing up straight and going through the front door.

Nathan was still in the sitting room, glaring at the window like it had done something to personally affront him.

"You done?" he asked, voice gruff. Right, maybe not the best time to press him.

"For now, yes. I was wondering if there's anything you'd like me to cook for you. I have to take a trip into the city tomorrow so I might as well swing by."

He stared at her again, and she couldn't tell if he was glaring at her or it was just the way his scars pulled at one of his eyes. But she held steady and casual, like she couldn't care less what he answered.

"...I wouldn't mind some meatloaf," he muttered eventually, his gaze finally breaking and going back to the window.

"Meatloaf it is!"

8

Nathan

$\mathcal{H}$e could call the sheriff or just tell her to back off, and yet he didn't when the giant woman showed up again for the third day in a row, dressed in her clunky over-alls and a different tank top. It stuck out less than her fancy dress and retro look, but she was still so pretty, so clean and flawless that she made everything about his property look dingy in comparison.

And he hated it.

Nathan was fully aware that she wasn't what would be considered classically pretty in the modern day and age, her hips too wide and her belly too soft, but there was no denying she had a retro sort of gorgeousness to her. From the heart shape of her face to her generous curves, even to her thick, styled hair. If she was anyone else, maybe he'd want to run his fingers through it, but since she was some sort of beautiful-but-persistent intruder to his house, he shoved that feeling far, far away.

"I noticed you have a lovely garden out front, between the raised beds and some tilled patches, but there's not a ton planted. Are you giving the earth a break?"

For a split second he was surprised at her question, but then he remembered that she had a ranch of her own and probably spent tons of her time in a garden—especially going by the interesting produce that Ol' Papa Miller shared with the town.

"I haven't really had the time or energy since the accident, so I've had to pick about three beds to maintain and that's it. I haven't even been able to amend the soil."

Nathan's eyes widened as he finished his sentence. He hadn't planned on admitting how much he'd been failing, but the words had just popped out like they had a mind of their own.

"Oh. Well, why don't I just finish that for you since I'm here? Where's your compost?"

Nathan narrowed his eyes, suspicion lancing through him. "Didn't you have to get to the city?"

"Not for several hours, actually. It's a night thing."

"Is that so?"

She nodded, although she didn't make eye contact. He'd had a feeling that she was lying as an excuse to come around, but he wasn't going to press her on it.

"I actually don't have much of a compost pile anymore," he answered. "With everything that's been going on, I haven't been able to maintain it." Another admission of his own weakness. Why didn't he just put a helpless sign on his chest and lay down on the floor?

Didn't she find you laid out on the floor already though?

Nathan brushed off that thought with gritted teeth and tried to continue on like he wasn't going through his own personal crisis. "Besides, it's a lot of work to amend my whole garden."

"I know. I don't imagine I can get it done in just a few hours, but I could come by tomorrow and the day after, probably."

There was that irritation again, welling up in him and stinging his pride. "Even if you magically found compost and amended the whole thing, it wouldn't be like I could actually maintain it. It'd all just go to waste."

But she sent him another one of those blinding smiles. "Don't worry, we can plant it together. I don't mind helping at all."

"Yeah, that much is clear."

"Hmm? What was that?"

"Nothing."

"Oh, okay. Anyway, we have plenty of extra compost back home. I'll bring in some tomorrow and start to work on that."

The anger began to bubble up inside him and once more, words butted out of his mouth without his permission.

"You know, you're being real assumptive here. You don't have a right to just barge into my house and tell me what's what, and you don't have a right to just tell me that we're going to work on a garden together. I—Are you even listening to me?"

The entire time he was talking, Clara had been walking to her Jeep and unloading more bags and buckets like he wasn't even saying anything at all. While Nathan wasn't exactly in the habit of chewing people out, they usually had the decency to at least listen to him when he did.

"Of course, I'm listening," she said, completely casual, like he wasn't trying to scathingly tell her to get off his property.

"And!?"

He felt like he was in a parallel universe, where nothing made sense and strange people just erupted into other people's houses like unwelcome fairy godparents to clean and grant wishes.

And cook you delicious meals, his mind supplied.

"And I'm going to go clean your bathroom once I set your meal in the kitchen. I hope you like the meatloaf. It's my mother's recipe."

Like he wasn't just yelling at her, she gathered her things in her arms and headed inside. Nathan strode after her, leaving his chair on the lawn. Clara was completely serene as she set another fancy meal container on his counter.

"You'll have to tell me what you think," she said with such a sweet look that Nathan momentarily forgot what he was angrily yelling at her for.

Her grin growing, she lifted the lid and he was instantly hit with a nearly overwhelming delicious smell. Savory, rich and welcoming, it made his mouth instantly water. He'd been eating her delicious roast for pretty much every meal for the past two days, so he wasn't even that hungry, and yet the smell was sinfully tempting.

"I'm guessing by the expression on your face that you like it so far," she said with a small laugh.

"Smells great," Nathan managed to croak.

"Fantastic."

That sweet look of hers turned into a wink, and Nathan had absolutely *no* idea what to think of that. It was like his brain whited out and all that was left was static. Rich women didn't wink at him. Beautiful women didn't wink at him. At best, women saw his scars or his trembling hands and just looked at him with pity.

But not Miss Clara Miller

"Right, I'll leave you to it. Just help yourself." Then she was already heading towards his bathroom, leaving him sputtering in his kitchen.

Well, he could finish chewing her out later. That meatloaf did smell awful good after all, and it would be a real sin to waste it.

9

Nathan

"You've really made some excellent progress here, Nathan. I've noticed you have more energy, and the blood work you came in for yesterday shows much less anemia and general better nutrition. Has something about your living situation changed?"

Had something changed? That was one way of putting it. It'd been a solid month since that strange, painfully gorgeous Clara woman started pestering him, and there was a long, long list of things she'd helped get done.

Nathan still resented her, but he resented her in the same way he resented his body, or the lightning, or the scars that ached and made his skin feel so tender. They were unavoidable realities that he just had to deal with. At least with Clara, she was a helpful sort of calamity.

She brought him two meals a week at least and often plenty

of groceries for easy-to-make meals when he was too exhausted to move. She'd helped amend the garden, hauled in enough compost to restart his own pile, and about a billion and one other things. And although he'd probably never admit it, he was eternally grateful to her.

"I've had a little more help back at home, and I guess you can say that I've been eating more regularly. And real meals, not the frozen stuff you get on my case about."

Alejandro smiled, nodding his head exactly how one would expect a doctor to. "That's excellent to hear. By all means, please keep it up. It's very obvious that it's doing wonders for you."

Nathan couldn't remember the last time the doctor had said something so hopeful, and he found himself licking his lips. "Wonders, huh?"

"Yes. Now, don't go doing cartwheels out in the lot, but I'm happy with this improvement."

What was that flickering in Nate's belly? It was warm and fizzing, almost foreign in its effervescence. Was that... hope? He'd forgotten what that felt like. "Does... Is it..." he swallowed hard. "Does this mean there's a chance I could go back to normal?"

It took all of Nathan's strength to lift his gaze and look Alejandro in the face. He was afraid of the answer, afraid of what it would mean for his life, and yet he knew he *had* to see what passed across his doctor's visage.

And much to his disappointment, Alejandro didn't answer right away. In fact, he didn't answer for almost a full minute. To be honest, that was a reply all on its own.

"Oh..." It was like someone had punched all of the air out of Nathan's lungs, which wasn't a great thing considering how often he had trouble breathing.

"Look, Nathan, let's not be negative about this—"

"Not negative?" Nathan heard himself snap, but it felt like he was outside of his own body and it was functioning on its own. "How can I be not negative!? You're telling me that my entire life could just be this... this sort of miserable nonexistence!?"

"No, I'm telling you it's impossible to say. Some people who are struck by lightning fight with lung problems and dizziness their entire life. Some recover and don't experience anything beyond soreness and occasional inflammation. The only things we know are that rest, upkeep, support and positivity make huge differences."

"What, so I'm just supposed to happy my way out of this mess?"

"No, that's not what I'm saying. Mr. Westbrook, you are in pain. Your body is recovering from being hit with enough energy to fry you from the inside out. You will have bad days, awful days and even worse days, days that have you in tears, lying in bed or on the floor and wishing everything would just stop."

"Geez, don't make it sound like so much fun."

"But the important thing is that you recognize that those days are only temporary, and each one will be a little less awful than the last. Not to be on the nose, but thinking of them as storms to weather instead of a permanent fixture of your life can do wonders." He paused a moment, seeming to think. "Like the meals, like whoever has been helping you with chores at home, it's the littlest things that matter to our soul and our psyche."

Nathan didn't say anything to that, his whole body feeling like it deflated. What Alejandro said made sense, but part of him didn't want to listen to it. That part of him just wanted to yell some more, maybe throw something, and stew in his misery.

Maybe that was the part of him he should listen to a lot less. It certainly never actually made him feel any better.

Then again, what did Alejandro know? He was a rich, able-bodied and dashingly handsome *doctor*. What kind of pain had he ever gone through? He was even dating the eldest Miller girl, meaning he was going to get even more filthy rich.

"I'll keep that in mind," he managed to grunt out.

"Excellent. Remember, I'm here for you, Nathan. Whatever you need."

"Right."

"Don't forget to stop with the receptionist outside and set up your next check-up. Is there anything else you need?"

"Nah. I'm good."

"Alright. Be well, Mr. Westbrook. And don't hold back on calling me if you need anything, really."

"I'm not much of one for talking on the phone," was all Nathan said before using his cane to walk himself out.

He held himself together as he did indeed set up his next appointment, then drove further into town for his various prescriptions and vitamins. Even the ride home was relatively uneventful. And concentrating on the road gave him a break from the anger and frustration boiling inside him.

When he'd first woken up from his medical coma, he hadn't quite believed them when they said what had happened. But now that he was a year out from the accident, it was so easy to get it. There was a before-lightning Nathan and an after-lightning Nathan, and after-lightning Nathan was a miserable, angry mess.

Why had God done this to him? He couldn't blame another human. It wasn't like someone had robbed him, hit him with a car or had used malice to hurt him. No, he'd been literally struck down in a freak accident.

By the time he finally pulled into his drive, he was simmering with all that displaced rage, with the unfairness of it all. Seething, Nathan stormed into his house, slamming the door into place. But that wasn't enough.

He didn't know if anything would ever be *enough.*

Letting out an angry cry, his cane dropped to the floor as he stumbled forward, reaching for the closest picture frame on the wall and flinging it to the floor. Glass shattered and the frame made quite a racket as it bounced, giving him the slightest sliver of satisfaction.

More, he needed *more.* His anger was rushing so white and hot through him that he felt he might explode with it.

Another picture frame. A hunting trophy. His fishing license. But it wasn't until he reached for one of the shelves he had in the hall that he lost his balance and toppled backward.

Nathan tried to catch himself, spitting curses as he tumbled, but that only sent him careening into the wall.

"Umph!" All of the breath was driven out of him with the collision and a searing pain sliced right through his arm. Looking down, he saw his skin had split right next to his deepest scars, the impact clearly severing what little healing he'd done.

It was a hairline welt, barely even bleeding, but it stung something fierce. Biting and intense, it reminded him that he was basically Frankenstein, cobbled together pieces of flesh and grafts from a team of doctors in the city. He'd been a man once.

But now, he was just a monster.

10

Clara

Clara hummed to herself as she walked up to Nathan's house, a full meal in a basket under one of her arms and a homemade pie in the other.

She'd really outdone herself this time, she was fairly sure, and she was plenty excited for Mr. Westbrook to come to the door. Not that he would ever show actual excitement, but she was sure that underneath his gruff exterior that he appreciated what she did. He kept letting her come over, after all.

But still... after two months, she thought that her natural charm would have rubbed off on him a little more, but Nathan was just as prickly as when she'd arrived. Surly, short and taciturn, sometimes she felt as if he hated her. But other times, like when they were setting up his garden together or starting his seedlings, she saw glimpses of someone else underneath. Someone kind, who loved the earth and loved his animals. It was a shame he was buried under so much bitterness, but it wasn't like Clara didn't get why.

"Nathan?" she called after he didn't answer for a minute. Sometimes he took a bit to get to the door, but he rarely took so long without calling out to her. Although he was gruff, she could tell that he tried to be at least a little polite. "Nathan, it's me, Clara."

Still no answer, and there went the hairs on the back of her neck. Sure, Nathan was surly, maybe even mean occasionally, but he always answered his door.

"Nate, I'm coming in!"

Setting her food down just like that fateful first visit, she jiggled the handle. It opened, not locked but only partially stuck, it seemed, and Clara was so focused on getting in that she didn't even stop to think about what might be waiting for her on the other side.

She wasn't quite sure what she expected. Maybe him on the floor again, maybe something worse, but it certainly wasn't for his house to be an absolute wreck.

Sure, Mr. Westbrook was a bachelor and had always had a bit of clutter and mess, but what Clara was staring at wasn't just a *mess*. No, it was like a tornado had gone down his hall, yanking pictures off the wall and tipping over shelves alike, leaving glass and debris scattered everywhere.

"Nathan?" Clara called again, fear coursing through her. Had he been robbed? It was well known in town what kind of condition he was in, but she hadn't thought anyone would ever want to take advantage of that. But what else—

"Oh, is you a'gin," a slurred voice came from the living room. Clara didn't visit that space often, as it felt very much like Nathan's private space, only vacuuming it a couple times and dusting once, but she walked there now.

"Nathan, are you alright? Did something happen?"

"Wha' a man can't redecorate his own house in peace?"

Clara rounded the corner to find Nathan slumped on his couch, a bottle of what look liked whisky in his hand and complete destruction all around him. Very clearly, the man was drunk as a skunk.

"Mr. Westbrook, you've made quite a mess while I was gone," she remarked cautiously, taking in everything about the scene.

He was wearing different clothes since she had last seen him, but considering she'd last visited on Saturday and he had a doctor's appointment on Monday, that meant he could have been like this anywhere from one to three days. That... that couldn't be good. His hair was greasy atop his head and he looked incredibly pale.

"Iz my house, giant lady. I do what I want!"

Maybe she should have been irritated. Maybe she should have judged him. But Clara was acutely reminded of the one time Cass had a complete meltdown during her first week at home. She'd screamed, thrown things at her door and even cursed Papa out. It had been frightening, for sure, but a call to the doctor had been quite illuminating. Between coming off her higher levels of pain medication, dealing with all the reminders of her own life and handling her PTSD from the accident, it was completely normal for Cass to have some missteps and breakdowns. The important thing was that they needed to be rare and decrease in frequency as she healed.

And they had. Cass rarely ever had outbursts in the past few months, and when she did, she always apologized. But that was after a year of the full support of her family. As far as Clara could tell, Nathan didn't have anyone.

"I can see that," Clara said levelly. "Have you had anything to eat lately?"

Nathan looked at her with red-rimmed eyes and goodness, if there wasn't so much sadness and anger in that gaze. There was far too much pain in the man, and Clara wished he would let her help a bit more.

"I... I finished the stuff you made last time. S'good."

"I'm glad you liked it. I brought you more food and a pie. Can your stomach handle some of that?"

That gaze of his narrowed in a way that was entirely Mr. Westbrook. "You're being so nice."

"Am I not usually?"

"No," he groused, melting further into his couch. "You're always so nice. It's annoying."

Clara laughed. It probably wasn't a normal response, but she couldn't help it. "Would you believe that's not the first time I've heard that?"

"Oh yeah? You just been a real martyr yer, uh... yer whole life, huh?"

"No, but after my mother died, I think I learned a whole lot about community and helping others. My family wouldn't have made it if several people in the town hadn't come and cooked for us, cleaned for us, prayed with us."

That seemed to jolt the man and he shifted uncomfortably in his seat. "I forgot your mama died."

"That's alright. It was over a decade ago. Did you even live in the town then?"

"No... no, I dinnit. I moved here maybe... five years ago, I think? No. Six. Yeah, six."

"Exactly. So, don't worry about it. All I need you to do is think about if you can handle food right now or if you want me to help you up to your room for some real rest."

"I... I could eat."

"Alright then, I'll go get you a plate and a glass of water."

He nodded dully, looking more miserable than ever. Clara pitied him, she did, and her heart ached. There was just so much pain there, layered in his scars, in his heart and in his soul. Although Clara knew she couldn't fix everything, she desperately wished she could reach into him and yank all that agony out.

Just like with Cass, she knew it took time, patience and support. But what kind of support could she give when he wouldn't let her in? Sure, she made her way into his house just fine, but he always kept her at a distance, both emotionally and physically. She could tell he was scarred, but she'd never gotten a good look at them. He always wore long sleeves and pants and would constantly angle his face away from her. When he couldn't, he made sure he was six feet or more away. In fact, the only time they had ever been physically close was when she had helped him up into his chair on their first meeting, and then she'd been too shocked about the whole situation to actually get a good look at him.

Oh well. It wasn't something that was likely to change anytime soon, so Clara busied herself with making Nathan a small plate and a glass of water. When she reached the living room, he was already dozing against the back of the couch, so she set it down beside him and took the bottle of whiskey that had nearly sunken into the threadbare cushions.

"I think you're going to need to go on vacation for a little bit," she told the bottle as if it could hear her. It didn't take long to squirrel it away into a back corner of a kitchen cabinet, and then she went about cleaning up the worst of the mess.

It wasn't easy, that was for sure, especially with all the glass scattered around. But Clara played music softly from her phone and took breaks to both feed the pigs and go visit with the chickens. She was surprised to see that they'd all been fed, which meant that Nathan's drunkenness was recent, or he'd stumbled out to take care of his flock even when he was inebriated.

Honestly, Clara wouldn't have been surprised if it was the latter. Clearly, he loved his birds more than he liked actual humans. Clara wondered if something had happened to him to make him such a loner or if he'd always been that way.

Oh well, it wasn't like she was going to find out while he was unconscious. And who knew, maybe after getting some of his misery out of his system, he would actually feel like telling her.

Clara wasn't going to hold her breath for that, of course.

No, she was just going to clean, keep bringing him meals, and help him with his garden plots and his animals. And if that was all that he would ever let her do, and if he never opened up to her, well that would just have to be the way it was.

The hours slipped by quickly and before Clara knew it, night was beginning to fall, the coral-bright rays of the sun dissipating into the cooler colors of twilight. Wiping her forehead, she returned to the living room to see Nathan still asleep.

"You must have needed your rest," she told him even though she knew he wasn't going to reply. Looking around, she spotted an old quilt folded on his recliner and picked it up, draping it across his long form. And for the first time since she'd met him, she had a chance to look at him. Really, actually *look.*

She had known that part of his face was scarred, starting at the right side of his hairline, going down the side of his face and then his neck, but she'd never studied it directly because that would have been just about the rudest thing she could have done. But she was surprised to see that his damaged flesh wasn't anything like Cass's. Not at all. Instead, it was... well it was almost like plant roots, tracing across his skin in delicate little patterns, some swirling around each other and some of them in jagged lines like... like...

"Like lightning," Clara breathed to herself.

She knew it was inappropriate, in fact, a voice inside of her screamed for her to just excuse herself from the house and leave, and yet her hand came up to his face, one finger gently tracing over the filigree of his skin.

"Huh."

It was almost beautiful, if that made any sense at all. Like some sort of artist had deliberately tattooed the pattern on his skin. Clara had never known that a human could be marked so, even by lightning, and her brain began to itch to find out more, more, *more* about exactly what Nathan's body was doing to him.

Even if that really, *really* wasn't her place.

Clearing her throat, Clara jolted to her feet. What was that saying about keeping one's hands to oneself? She should probably listen to that and move along.

After a moment more of studying his features and the borderline mystical scars that traveled across them, she hurried to get him a couple of bottles of water from the fridge, some headache and stomach medicine from his upstairs bathroom, then a bucket for...well, just in case.

But when all that was said and done, she found herself wanting to linger. She'd always been a curious one, wanting to figure out how things worked or were put together. That was one of the reasons she loved sewing so much. A back part of her brain wanted to push down the collar of Nathan's oversized shirt and see what was underneath. Did those strange, lightning-like markings cover his chest? His stomach? Were they bigger? More vibrant?

"Geez, girl. Get a grip," Clara hissed to herself, shaking her head and hurrying toward the door. She had definitely crossed some boundaries she probably shouldn't have, and she chided herself all the way out to her car. She knew from Cass how important it was to respect the privacy of someone who was injured or in need of her help, so why was she so tempted to toe over that line?

She didn't know, and answers didn't come as she drove. She could only wonder if she was even doing the right thing by Nathan or if she was only caught up in her own need to be a do-gooder.

Ugh. When had being charitable gotten so messy?

11

Nathan

Nathan woke up sick as a dog. For several long, long minutes there was nothing but pain and nausea. For a fleeting moment, he once again thought he was back in the hospital, but then blurry reality came sweeping back to him.

Oh.

Right.

He had most definitely drunk himself silly. He couldn't remember the last time he'd done something like that. Alcohol was generally not recommended for his recovery, and being stone-cold drunk was *definitely* not a part of the plan.

At least there was no one to tattle to Alejandro about his mini bender.

Groaning, Nathan sat up and his hand knocked against

something, sending it tumbling into his lap. Only after a lot of blinking did he realize it was a water bottle.

"Hey, where did this come from?" he croaked, lifting it with shaking hands and unscrewing the top. The cool liquid felt amazing across his tongue, and for a moment he just sat there and basked in the refreshing deluge.

But after a few moments of quiet, his bladder announced its displeasure with him, and Nathan realized he needed to get up *immediately*. Too bad his body wasn't quite coordinated enough to react quickly, and he struggled for much longer than he would like to admit getting up onto his feet.

After one trip to his downstairs half bathroom and back, he finally noticed that there was a bucket beside where his head had been, and he'd had to extricate himself from his old quilt. He didn't remember ever grabbing it from the chair it always sat in, and that, along with the bucket, made him think that he hadn't quite been alone.

Clara.

Nathan felt his one good cheek color red, embarrassment lancing through him. Clara had seen him drunk? And not just regular, havin' a good time drunk, but sloppy, messy, *drunk-drunk*.

How mortifying.

Nathan hated being weak, and he hated that she saw him like that. Most of all he didn't want her to think he was some lazy, alcoholic bum who drank himself into a stupor every time he got a little sad. He didn't know *why* it was so important to him that she not think that, but it was.

He needed to clean up. He needed to clean up, get some food in himself, some water and pull himself out of the hole he was in. He needed—

Knock, knock!

He needed that *not* to be Clara at his door.

Nathan stood there a moment, as if he could will away whoever was on the other side of his door. But then the knock sounded again, echoing the pounding of his own skull.

The next thing he knew, he was striding to the front of his house, walking straighter and quicker than he had in ages. He didn't know where he got the air into his lungs, but the next words out of his mouth escaped in a loud bellow.

"Go away!"

"Ah, Mr. Westbrook, you're up. How are you feeling?"

Her tone was light, pleasant through the door, and that just made Nathan's temper ramp up that much more. He was *mean* to her, rude and short and perpetually unpleasant. Why was she pretending that he wasn't an unlikable curmudgeon? They both knew he was awful.

"Why are you here? Looking for an encore after the last time?"

"No, not really. Just came to do some chores, that's all."

She was so calm, no hitch in her voice, just a matter-of-fact sort of cadence. *How* could she talk to him so breezily?

"Would you just leave me alone? We both know I'm not worth all this trouble!"

She started to say something but then cut herself off. For the briefest of moments, he thought maybe she'd finally hit her limit, but then her calm voice was drifting through his door again.

"You had a bad night, Mr. Westbrook, that's all. I'm sure your hangover is unpleasant enough. You don't need to punish yourself further."

"What... what do you know about it?"

Despite his objection, her words rang true to him, hitting him square in the chest and making all of his defenses rise. Without thinking, his hand shot forward, locking the door.

"I don't know what kind of martyr complex you have, but I don't need it. I don't need any of your charity!"

"Charity is my older sister, actually. I'm Clara, so you don't have to worry about that."

"Really? You're going to make a pun about your family's weird names *now*?"

"They're not weird. They're just an alliteration."

"Go away, Clara!"

Despite the steel in his voice, she didn't waver, didn't tell him off. She just let out a quiet sigh and he heard her step back.

"Alright, I'll do some of your chores out here, then go home. You feel better, Nathan."

Wait... the fight was over? It didn't even really feel like a fight, Clara being far too kind and deferential. Weren't the Miller girls supposed to be prickly or something? He felt like he'd heard as much about the older two.

But not Clara, apparently. Not perfect, beautiful Clara. He could see from his window that she was already heading towards his chicken coop, whistling to herself all the while.

Ridiculous.

Anger churning in his gut, Nathan stormed to his fridge and grabbed another beer from it. Somewhere, deep within himself, a voice told him that he wasn't actually mad at Clara, only himself, but that voice didn't need to be listened to.

Cracking open the top, Nathan went to take a long chug. But before a single drop could land in his mouth, a terrible shrieking sound ripped through the air just outside his house.

For the second time in a day, he found himself striding toward the front of his home much more quickly than he probably should have. But he didn't have the time to question that because somehow, a coyote had gotten into his pigpen and was trying to go after one of his younglings.

"No!"

Adrenaline shot through Nate as he rushed for his rarely used guns. Coyotes normally didn't come onto his land. It smelled too much of humans and his animals were always well protected.

Although, apparently not protected enough.

Cursing his uneven steps, Nathan made it back to his porch and started loading his gun, shouting out to try to scare the creature away. But the pigs were making such a racket, he doubted the little predator could even hear him.

The thing was, he knew that his pigs would probably overwhelm and tear the coyote apart, but some could get injured. And it would be so easy to lose a little one. Nathan put so much work into those pigs, spending years cultivating a nice, small herd that gave reliable offspring for meat, he wasn't about to have a *coyote* mess that all up.

But before he could get a single bullet in, suddenly Clara was sprinting by him, an overall-clad streak across the lawn. Without missing a beat, she literally vaulted over the side of the pen, landing right next to the cornered piglet.

"Get outta here!" she cried, her voice louder and harsher than Nate had ever heard her. Naturally, the coyote was fairly concerned at the giant that landed just in front of him, and that concern clearly shot up to terror as she batted at it with a broom. "You run off now and tell all your friends how bad this place is!"

Nathan watched, jaw practically falling down to his chin,

as the coyote yelped then snarled, lunging forward just for Clara to bat it away again, screaming unintelligible noises at it. In the back of his mind, Nathan knew she was trying to intimidate it with noise and confusion rather than hurting it—a broom wasn't exactly a lethal weapon—and surprisingly, it worked. The coyote tucked tail and ran, slinking out of the tiny little furrow it had dug under Nate's protective wire on the inside of his fence. He was definitely going to have to fix that.

But even with the attacker gone, it was still chaos in the pen, and Clara's screaming didn't help that. Pigs were running every which way, kicking up mud to impressive heights. Maybe it would have even been a bit comical with the danger gone if it weren't for the massive mama pig rushing for Clara.

"Watch out!" Nate called, lurching forward. Clearly the sow thought Clara was a threat, and that definitely wasn't good. "Clara, get out of there!"

In all his life, Nate didn't think he'd ever seen a big woman move so incredibly fast. She dashed from the mud that she had landed in to the dry part of the pen—only falling once—then vaulted over the fence *again*. As impressive as her first one had been, it was even more astounding to see her do it while covered in mud and filth with an angry pig chasing her.

She landed in a crouch, holding her arms out to steady herself, and when she stood, Nate didn't miss how her legs were trembling slightly. After what seemed like an age, her eyes flicked to his, and they both stared at each other in silence.

Strangely, after so much noise, the world seemed to go kind of quiet, just her and him as their minds caught up with everything that had happened. He'd been so *mean* to her. So mean. And still she'd...

Wiping the mud that was coating her hands onto her pants,

Clara drew in a long breath. "I think it's time for me to head home now, Mr. Westbrook. You have a nice day."

And then she was heading towards her Jeep and driving off, leaving Nate to wonder if that had really happened or if he was having his first hangover-induced hallucination.

12

Nathan

He couldn't get the image of Clara facing off against that coyote out of his head. Whenever he was idle, it would play over again, like his mind was trying to analyze every single facet of it. By the time the next day rolled around, it had turned into something out of some sort of dramatic movie in his mind's eye. Ridiculous.

But also... still pretty cool.

Without really acknowledging it, Nathan found himself waiting for her to show up for lunch as she usually did. Maybe he could joke with her, thank her for doing that without sounding too pathetic. He could have handled the coyote with his gun, of course. She hadn't needed to literally put herself in harm's way.

She didn't need to, and yet she did anyway.

Huh.

Swallowing hard, Nathan found himself looking at the clock. She was late, which was unusual for her. He'd always assumed her persistence went hand in hand with punctuality. Apparently not.

Nathan's foot bounced as he continued to wait for Clara's arrival, something that his body hadn't really done since before the accident. Probably something he should make note of, but his mind kept going to the ticking of the clock and the minutes flying by. But finally, three hours after her usual arrival time, Nathan had to admit to himself that she wasn't coming.

Huh.

Strange how, after all his yelling at her to go away, he was surprised that she wasn't at his door. She'd become such a constant in his life in the two months that she'd been showing up. He almost didn't know what to do without her. The house was strangely quiet without her, like his brain was expecting to hear her whistle or laugh floating through the rooms. Sure, he never talked to her much, only giving her begrudging answers, but that didn't... that didn't mean he didn't *listen.*

"This is silly. I'll just call her."

He dug into his pocket to pull out his phone, only to realize that he'd never bothered to learn her number.

Or her email.

Or *any* of her social media.

Oh. That... that probably was more telling than he would like to admit. He'd really stuck his foot in it, hadn't he? He'd complained about her help, taken her for granted, and then chased her off. And, as much as he'd like to blame her, he couldn't deny that it was entirely his fault. He'd *known* he was short with her; his whole goal had been to get her out of his hair and prove that he didn't need her. So... why did he suddenly feel like something was missing?

Oh well. It was probably for the better. He'd been alone ever since his mother had walked out of his life, and just because he was hit by lightning, that didn't mean that it was going to change.

"I... I suppose I should just make myself something to eat." Better than moping about, at least.

But as Nathan went through making himself some toast, he found himself looking at his empty sink and then his clean kitchen floor, and then thinking about his very full fridge. Clara, in all her generosity and persistence, had really integrated herself into his home. He could see her standing at his sink, hear the thump of her shoes as she went upstairs to clean his bathroom or fetch his bedding for washing. Without her... how was he going to keep up with everything? Was he just going to fall back to how bad it had been before? Because it had been *so* bad.

Why had he been so mean to her? What was the point?

Nathan slammed his fist on the counter, knocking the plate that he'd put the toast on to the floor.

"Why do I keep doing this to myself?"

Tears began to well up, even though he shoved them down as hard as he could. He was *strong*. He was!

But why did it feel like there was a gaping hole under his feet that he could fall into at any moment? And why was he so full of anger that it felt like it was oozing out of all the awful scars covering his body? It was just so *much*, too much. How could God ask a single man to endure so much? Wasn't he supposed to not give more than one person could handle?

"The white flag is up, man!" Nathan yelled at his ceiling. "You can lay off, okay? I give up! *I give up!*"

There wasn't an answer.

There was never an answer. God didn't help people like

him. God helped martyrs like Clara and kind souls who didn't swear, didn't drink, and didn't terrorize people who were just trying to help them.

Nathan stood there in the silence, broken plate on the floor, toast growing cold, and he couldn't see it getting any better. His chest hurt so much it felt like it was going to crack in two, and he didn't even have Clara to distract him.

How was he going to maintain his garden? They'd planted so much of it, and it was going so well, but there was no way he could keep up. He was useless. So utterly useless.

The opposite of Clara, really. Who had been so impressive, standing out there in his pigpen, armed with only a broom and her sheer will. Who had been showing up for two months, with little gratitude from him, with a smile and a good spirit.

He couldn't say how long he stood there, listless and full of turmoil. An hour? Two? What did time matter anymore when he couldn't even stay awake a full day anyway? In the end, it took another heated conversation between two of his chickens to draw him out of the spiral he'd been sliding into.

"I might as well be productive if I'm going to be miserable." Besides, his homestead was all he had, his animals the only ones to stick by him even with his twisted, lightning-stricken form.

So, grabbing his pail from his porch, he went to at least try to tend to his chickens. Without them and his pigs, he really would be alone. And he supposed that he was finally ready to admit that the idea of being completely on his own terrified him.

13

Clara

Clara opened the oven door, basting the top of the Cornish hens once again. The delicious aroma filled the kitchen, but it still wasn't enough to take the edge off her nerves. Usually, making fancy things was her go-to when she was unsettled, but neither the pineapple rice nor the teriyaki glaze was helping her.

"Hey there, sunshine. It sure does smell delicious in here," Papa's voice clearly drifted to her as he strolled over to the fridge.

Clara merely grunted in response, standing up from the oven and setting her baster to the side. She just felt so... well, she didn't quite have the words for it. It just wasn't a nice feeling.

"You know," Papa said slowly, regarding her while he slowly

drank from the tea he'd poured. "I noticed the bathroom upstairs is awfully messy."

Clara paused at that, recognizing the tone from her father immediately. It wasn't rude, or even reproachful, but it carried that curious sort of cadence that let her know that he was asking if something was up.

While Clara wasn't a total neat freak, she did like to keep the main bathroom spick-and-span because it had the best lighting in the house, so she often did her makeup and hair there. When she was a preteen, she used to leave eyeshadow and lipstick all over the place, along with errant strands of hair. But after her mother died and everything had fallen apart, she'd learned what a difference it made to keep the space tidy for everyone.

She hadn't cleaned up after herself that morning, not after doing victory curls and not after doing a full-face look that would have been fit for a high-concept photoshoot. And while Clara couldn't say exactly why, she just hadn't had it in her to stay in that bathroom and put everything away. In fact, her fingers were itching to wipe her entire face off and do a whole new look and maybe even change her dress.

"Honey, you alright over there?"

Oh, she had been standing there silently for several long moments, hadn't she? "I... I suppose there was a bit of an incident at Nathan's."

"An incident?" Papa Miller immediately straightened. "He didn't—"

"No! Nothing like that! I just... it made me think that maybe I'm not doing the right thing. I feel like I'm crossing all these boundaries of his, and I don't want to be a bully."

Papa relaxed, but there was still a concerned expression

across his face. "Well, you know what they say about a horse being led to water. Try as you might, you can't force that thing to drink. I know it's hard for you, but if he doesn't want your help after all this time together, it's not your job to save him."

So much easier said than done. Clara sighed, letting all of the air leave her before drawing in another breath. "I know. It's just, well, I feel bad for him. He's in so much pain. I can see it in everything he does. I want him to be happy, and I don't want his animals to suffer because he's sick."

"Aw, sweetheart, come here."

Papa Miller opened his arms and Clara went right to him, hugging him with all she had. As the second tallest of his children, she was almost his height, but that didn't stop her from embracing him like she was still a young girl. She didn't know where she would be without Papa. His kindness, his understanding, she truly felt awful for her southern cousins who struggled so much with their own father, because Papa was her rock.

"You've always had such a big heart, and I understand you don't want anyone to hurt how you had to hurt after Mama passed, but you can't save everyone."

"I know Papa, I know." Clara hadn't expected to cry. She hadn't even known that she was that upset, but suddenly the tears were trickling out of the corner of her eyes and a couple of sobs hitched out of her throat.

"There, there, my little gardener. You keep on having that big heart. The world needs more people like you."

Clara nodded, letting herself ride through the sudden crests of emotions within her. But she couldn't help but think, as wonderful and safe as her father's arms were, that Nathan didn't have anything like that.

Nathan didn't have a single soul.

She didn't know what had happened to him, what had led him to be alone in that house. Had it just been the lightning? Had something else happened? She'd always wanted to ask, but that seemed like quite the personal question, and she never got past pleasantries with Nathan.

Actually... things never even got to 'pleasant' if she was truthful.

Pulling away from Papa, Clara wiped her face, her father gently patting her cheek when she was done. She felt marginally more composed with all of that out of her, the anxiety settling down into the pit of her stomach. Not gone entirely, but much more manageable than it had been.

"Thanks, Papa. You always know what to say."

"Hardly. But I've been through some things in my time."

"Because you're so old?"

"Hey, not too old to bend you over my knee."

"I think your leg might give out."

"*Clara.*"

"Yeah, yeah, I'm fine, Papa. Thank you. Really."

"No problem, sunshine. Have you decided what you're going to do?"

"I... I don't know. I'm worried that I might make a decision that disappoints you."

"I understand, sunshine. The choice is yours, and I support you no matter what."

Clara grinned again, her heart squeezing ever so gently in her chest. It was wonderful to know that even if she made a mistake, her father wouldn't judge her.

"Thank you, Papa. That means the world to me."

The last of the tears gone, Clara straightened herself and

returned to her Cornish hens. They still smelled amazing, but she found that she didn't need them to be as perfect as she had a few minutes earlier.

She had a lot to think about, that was for certain, but she felt comfortable enough to take her time and figure things out.

14

Nathan

A week.

A *whole* week.

Seven days and Clara still hadn't shown up. Nathan knew that he needed to come to terms with the fact that she wasn't ever coming back, but he kept finding himself looking towards the dirt road leading up to his cabin, hoping that he might see the dust her Jeep always kicked up along the way.

But no, his driveway remained empty and his fridge was growing emptier by the minute. He would need to go into town soon or call his church connection to get another batch of groceries dropped off to him.

But if he did that, they would have to know that he'd chased Clara off, if they didn't know already, and he was pretty embarrassed by the whole thing.

His stomach twisted at that, sending a wake of nausea for a

while. Nathan paused in his walkthrough of his garden, trying to breathe in through his nose and out through his mouth. He probably shouldn't have been outside when he wasn't feeling his best, but the garden was fully amended and the starters that he and Clara had planted were long since ready to go into the ground.

The world bucked below him, nearly sending him to his knees, and Nathan barely caught himself from pitching right over.

"Whoa there, whoa. I need to sit down."

Stumbling forward, he tried to make it to his porch, only to get so winded that he gagged and ended up doubled over to throw up.

"This... this isn't good."

It wasn't, and when he somehow made it to his porch, the entire world spinning around him, he realized that he hadn't eaten since the day before.

Uh-oh.

Hands shaking, Nathan ran a hand through his hair. It was far too long, but it wasn't like he was going to haul himself into town to get it cut. Especially since he couldn't bring himself to go into town for groceries or anything else that was far more vital.

Eventually, the spinning and rippling earth stopped long enough for him to get to his feet and haul himself to his kitchen. Grabbing the closest thing—a banana—he ripped the peel off and practically shoved the whole thing into his mouth.

Geez, since when had his kitchen gotten so messy? And *how?* He couldn't remember the last time he cooked, and he'd basically been living off leftovers and toast since Clara had left.

A lot wasn't happening since Clara left. He was barely feeding his animals enough. The chicken's coop wasn't being cleaned properly, and he was sure he had eggs there that needed to be harvested. His starters were beginning to get root-bound, and the dust, dirt and grime were slowly seeping into his house again.

He... he needed to do something. He couldn't keep going on like he was just a miserable victim of a person who couldn't see the way out of his own misery. He needed *Clara*.

That feeling filled him with both embarrassment, anger, and a deep feeling of loneliness. He'd chased Clara off when she was possibly the best thing that had happened to him since his body had a lethal number of volts jolted through it.

He should have been grateful, should have been kinder, should have been less prideful and more receptive of her work. But he'd mistreated her until she'd gone away because her pureness, her *goodness,* just reminded him of the crotchety, ugly thing he'd become.

If he could, he would go right up to her house and beg for forgiveness. He knew he didn't deserve it, but at least *trying* would be an improvement instead of just laying back and rotting in lethargy. Or was it apathy? Nathan didn't know. Both seemed appropriate to the yawning chasm of darkness that was always hovering just over his shoulder.

Actually... he didn't know her address, but how hard would it be to find where she lived? After all, there was only one Miller ranch and most of the locals knew where it was. He was sure if he asked, someone would be more than happy to give him directions.

So the real question was, was he actually going to do something about his situation? Or was he still too scared?

15

Clara

When it rained, it certainly poured.

Mick, the ranch hand that Cass had hired, had been *incredibly* sick, so Clara had been using her extra time from not going to Nathan's to cover all the chores he wasn't able to do. The poor guy somehow managed to get viral meningitis. Clara felt absolutely awful for him.

She doubted he was going around making out with random people considering he was a rather introverted fellow, so she guessed he'd gotten it from drinking from a not-quite clean cup at the town's tavern. She never liked that place anyway and had especially loathed it since Cass's accident.

Speaking of Cass, her older sister seemed to be doing a great job taking care of the tall man. Clara could have been wrong, but she was fairly sure she noticed... something between the two. Not quite a spark, not quite as strong as a magnetic attraction, but there was a certain intensity whenever they were in a room together.

Who knew, maybe Charity wouldn't be the only Miller girl to fall in love.

"Wouldn't that be nice?" Clara sighed to herself as she swiped her feet across the mud-mat just beside the porch. She would *love* for Cass to find someone, especially someone who seemed to motivate her as much as Mick did. But also, she couldn't help but wish that there was someone for *her* out there.

But she'd long since given up on that. She'd never dated, never even had a kiss. She'd always been too fat, too tall, too broad, too *weird*. Folks in her family always told her she was beautiful, and when she went to the city in full glam, she got a few people who hit on her here or there. But most of the people in the town thought her retro look was bizarre, and most of society told her that her worth was measured by just how small her waist was.

It would be nice, for certain, to have someone look at her like Alejandro looked at Charity, or to feel that same intensity that there seemed to be between Mick and Cass, but it just wasn't in the cards. And that was fine with Clara. She'd rather be single and happy with herself then change for some man.

Someone cleared their throat and Clara jolted, nearly dropping her empty bucket as she jumped.

"Jiminy Cricket, you scared me!" she cried out, spinning to see none other than Mr. Westbrook standing in the center of her porch.

...what!?

Clara rubbed her eyes and sure enough, it was indeed Nathan, standing there with her roast pan and cover in his hands, looking quite bashful. She stared at him, and she knew she was staring, but she couldn't help but wonder what the heck he was doing there.

Did he really need to yell at her any more than he already had? She hadn't been around to tick him off for at least a week. She'd assumed that he would have been grateful that she'd finally gotten out of his hair, relieved that she'd dropped off the face of the earth.

She hadn't meant to ghost him. She'd been intending to call him and see if there was a better way she could meet his needs without crossing his boundaries so much. But with Mick being sick and Clara picking up the slack, she'd kind of let time fly by.

"I'm sorry for startling you," Nathan said, his voice uncertain and grating, like he wasn't quite sure how to speak. He was wearing a cowboy hat that partially shaded his face, a long-sleeved shirt with gardening gloves on and a pair of dark jeans. Pretty much the only part of his skin that was showing was a small sliver of his face, and even that was mostly hidden.

"It's fine. I know it wasn't intentional. I just wasn't expecting you."

He nodded, and it was quiet just long enough to be awkward. Clara didn't begrudge the man, even if he was so rude to her previously, but she didn't really understand why he was there or what he wanted.

Finally, he lifted the pan in a gesture. "It probably doesn't taste as nice as anything you can cook, but I made you something."

He... he cooked for her?

Clara continued to stare at him until he cleared his throat yet again. What, was that the third time? Goodness, where had all her manners gone? Apparently washed away by the deluge of confusion running through her.

"Um, would you like to come in and set it in the kitchen?"

He nodded jerkily, stepping to the side so that Clara could move past him. Which she did, after another moment's hesitation, leading him into her home.

No one was home, which wasn't unusual for when Clara took her first break from chores, somewhere between tending to the chickens and pruning the tomatoes, and she was momentarily grateful for that. It wasn't that she was ashamed of Mr. Westbrook, but after complaining about his behavior to some of her siblings, most of them had pretty ill opinions of the man.

"I hope you like it," he said lamely, eyes on the floor as he set it where she pointed on the counter.

"I'm sure I will," she answered, waiting until he stepped away to take the cover off. A delicious aroma almost immediately wafted up from it, and she found her mouth watering rather quickly. "Oh wow! That smells amazing. What is it?"

It looked like steak, but Clara was familiar enough with grilling to know that it wasn't. There were also potatoes, carrots and what looked like cauliflower, all soaked and roasted in the thick, aromatic gravy surrounding the meat.

"It's uh, venison. It's not the freshest, I bagged it during the last hunting season, but my meet freezer keeps it pretty well without getting burned."

"Wow, thank you, Mr. Westbrook. I..." That same confusion poured through her again, and Clara couldn't help but say the words rushing through her mind. "But uh, why?"

"Why?"

"Why this? Last we talked, you were quite upset with me and refused to let me into your house. This seems like quite the reversal in attitude."

"Ah yes, about that. I uh... I'm..." He faltered, but Clara didn't let him off the hook, maintaining her stare at him until he shifted and tried again. "I apologize for how I acted. It wasn't very nice of me. I've... I've been going through some stuff, but that's not an excuse. I'm sorry, Clara.

"And I'm not bribing you or nothin', but I was hoping maybe you could find it in you to forgive me and help me out again back on my homestead."

Clara's eyes shot open even wider. "You know, you say it's not a bribe, but I'm pretty sure plying me with delicious meals is pretty bribery."

The unscarred corner of his mouth quirked up ever so slightly. "Okay, maybe it is a little bit of a bribe."

Clara knew without a doubt that she was going to go back to help him; it was what her heart told her was right. But just because *she* knew that didn't mean she had to say that right away. Besides, she wanted to make sure he really meant what he said and wasn't going to go back to his old ways as soon as she was back on his property.

"Why would you want me back on your homestead? Seemed I just irritated you most of the time."

"You did," he answered plainly before turning a bright red. "I mean, I... yes, you irritated me because you were proof that I needed help. I've been on my own for so long that it made me feel weak and pathetic that I did. But I took out that irritation on you in a bad way, and I'm sorry. I don't like how I treated you, and I will try to be better, but I can't promise I won't slip up."

"But you need my help?" Clara repeated. Those words struck a chord in her, and she wanted to hear them again. Actually, she could hear them a dozen times over and that would be quite alright.

"I..." He sighed, rubbing his eyes then shifting from foot to foot.

Clara didn't enjoy seeing him so off-center, but she needed

affirmation that he didn't hate her and that she *was* actively helping his life.

But at the same time, hearing him admit why he'd been so mean made her heart ache. To know that he was embarrassed about his injury and that his pride smarted every time she helped him... well, it explained a lot.

"Yes. I need your help on the homestead."

"Alright then, I'll help you. But on one condition."

"Oh?" His one remaining eyebrow went up, disappearing into his long hair.

Hmm, he looked like he could use a trim. Had he even been to the town barber since she'd started helping him? She didn't think so.

"What's that?" he asked.

"I want you to go to church with me once a month."

He seemed surprised at that, but it made perfect sense to her. Clara was fairly certain that Nathan's self-isolation was hurting him. Being in a social situation like the breakfast hour before service or maybe even a small Bible study would probably do him good. Clara didn't think he had any friends, male or female, and that wasn't good for anyone.

"That's it? Church?"

"Yup. I hate going alone. And with Cass injured, Mick sick and everyone else busy, our schedules don't always sync up."

He didn't answer at first, his tongue coming out to lick his lips. Clara found herself following the movement perhaps a bit too keenly and instantly felt her cheeks burn. What was *that* about?

"Okay. I can do that."

And apparently it was that easy. Clara gave him a nod then offered her hand. "It's a deal then."

He looked down at her hand like it was something from

another planet. It was another long, awkward moment before he finally shook her hand, his glove rough against her skin. "It's a deal."

"Fantastic. Now, would you like something to eat? I just so happen to have some delicious roast right here on the counter."

16

Nathan

*L*ike no time had passed at all, Clara showed up right at lunch, another covered container in her hands. She was dressed in a pair of blue-black, polka-dotted overalls instead of her usual blue ones, and her hair was done up in twin buns atop her head. It was a good look for her, and Nathan found himself watching her the entire walk up the drive.

Oh... that was probably pretty creepy.

"Hello there," she said as she practically skipped up the stairs, grinning broadly at him. She wasn't wearing much makeup, only lipstick and something dark around her eyes, it seemed. Both of them emphasized her beautiful features and he couldn't help his gaze from flicking to them over and over again. "You ready to plot out the rest of the garden and get the seedlings organized for planting?"

"As ready as I'll ever be," he answered softly.

He hadn't expected her to be so kind or understanding when he'd visited her house. In fact, he'd almost expected her to slam the door right in his face. And she wouldn't have been wrong to do so, he knew that, but he was mighty glad she hadn't.

Instead, she smiled at him, invited him into her house, and even fed him some of the meal he'd made for her. He had been tempted to say no because he didn't want to be around if she hated his food, but turning her down seemed far too rude right after he'd just begged for her forgiveness.

She hadn't hated it, at least not that he could tell. She happily served the both of them and then even went back for seconds. People didn't get seconds of something they hated, right?

"Alright. Well, I'm gonna put another water bottle in the freezer to get cold while I work on this one, then we'll get to organizing!"

"Actually..." Nathan felt his cheeks burn vibrantly.

"What is it?"

"I could use some help with the animals."

"Oh, that's no problem. I'll do the water thing and then hop right on that. Why don't you grab a notebook and a pen for the garden?"

Nathan nodded and set about doing that, using his cane. He hadn't missed how his stamina had dropped considerably in the days since Clara left, and it was pretty shocking how much just one week back on his uneven diet had erased so much of his progress.

It seemed unfair to have to work so hard at just surviving, but he supposed that was the way the cookie crumbled when one was struck by lightning.

Thankfully—and mostly due to Clara's organizing his place

—he was able to find a notebook and pen quite quickly. He took it to their set-up spot in the garden but quickly realized that he didn't want to just wait there for the strong woman. He was feeling buoyed by her arrival, full of a sort of hopeful energy he hadn't had in ages, and he didn't want that to go to waste.

And maybe he was also a little worried that if he stayed in one place for too long, his ego would come sliding back in, biting and hissing that he didn't *need* Clara. That he wasn't really a man if he accepted her help.

Right, definitely better to help her with the chores.

Steeling himself, Nathan strode around to the side of his house to where his chickens lived. He'd half expected for Clara to have a pitchfork and to already be halfway through clearing the pen out, but instead she was crouched in the center of their pen, talking and gently petting several of them.

"Normally, my girls take a bit to warm up to people," he murmured, almost to himself. But Clara still jumped, the chickens around her feet clucking in disapproval.

"Do they?" Clara replied with a huff of a laugh as she smoothed out the front of her overalls. A nervous habit, it seemed. "I suppose it helps that I tend to bring them food." She knelt down again, and after a moment of reproach, the chickens once again started to surround her, having their own conversations and fights as they were wont to do.

"Yeah, they are pretty food motivated. Especially Rapunzel."

"Rapunzel, huh, let me guess. That's this little lady right here?" She pointed to his particularly fluffy Brahma chicken with a distinctive black spattering of feathers along one of her sides.

"How'd you know?"

"Because she was my first friend here and is the most likely to fight the others for a treat. She's got moxie."

"And a bottomless stomach," Nathan agreed with a laugh. He was aware that most people didn't give chickens much thought, even if they raised them, but he'd always been partial to his little flock. To him, they were the same as faithful dogs; they all had their own personalities and patterns that made them individuals.

Also, eggs were incredibly easy but valuable sources of protein.

"You know, I'm curious. I've been calling this lady Diva, but what's her real name?" She lifted up the smallest of his silkies, and Nathan couldn't help the sharp bark of laughter that punched out of him. "What? Did I say something funny?"

Nathan had to shake his head. "No, it's just... that's actually Lil' Diva that you're holding."

Her eyes went wide, and she too let out a breathless laugh. The sound surprised him, soft and genuine as it was, and he almost lost the thread of the conversation.

"No, you're kidding me!"

"I am absolutely not kidding you. Lil' Diva basically came out of the egg knowing she was all that and a bag of chips. Didn't have any other choice."

"Really?" She squinted at him suspiciously. "You're not pulling my leg?"

"I'm serious. Her name is Lil' Diva and always has been."

Another gentle laugh from Clara as she set the chicken down. Of course, Lil' Diva made a series of loud clucks until she was fed extra treats for being manhandled, but that was par for the course.

"I don't mean to make assumptions, but it's funny to me that someone like you would name one of their pretty chickies 'Diva.'"

"Someone like me, huh?" He murmured with a grin. She flushed at that, and he found he liked the way the pink color spilled across her cheeks before rushing down her neck. "And what exactly does that mean?"

She sputtered a moment, and it was far cuter than it probably should have been. "You know what I mean! Rugged, cowboy types. Independent manly man homestead bachelor. Need I go on?"

Oh, she was being nice. What she meant was scarred, decrepit, bitter cripples who can't handle even basic responsibilities.

"I guess I'm more of a multi-faceted individual than you thought."

"Well yeah, it's easier to see all those facets now that you're not covered in five feet of barbwire with titanium walls built all around you."

He huffed at that mental image, but she wasn't entirely wrong. "Yeah...sorry about that. I'm, uh, working on it."

She just waved her hand. "Don't worry about it. Now, tell me who this proud girl is."

He did, and then the next one, with her telling him about their personality or things they'd done. He hadn't realized that she's spent enough time with his flock to know them so well, especially since they weren't exactly overly fond of strangers.

"You must really like chickens," he noted finally.

"Oh, I'm just good with animals, I guess." She looked up from Miss Cinnamon-Binnamon III, who Nathan technically didn't even name.

"That much is apparent. What, was Dr. Dolittle your great uncle or something?"

She laughed, and Nathan couldn't help but wonder why he'd wasted so much time yelling at her when he could have had that pleasant sound escape those lips of hers instead.

"No, nothing like that. You just have to learn their language," she said.

"Their language?"

"Yeah, sure. Cats will blink at you slowly when they trust you, and they only meow at humans, really. Dogs will press against your legs for comfort or to sus out their hierarchy in your pack. Chickens will perp-perp over a good food supply or rebel yell. You learn how they talk, and it's like a whole new world is open to you."

Nathan didn't know what to say to that. Her words rang true, but he'd never heard it phrased that way. Sure, he knew when his chickens were saying that they were hungry, when they were mad at him for not giving them fresh garden pickings, and when they were squabbling like high school mean girls. But he'd never thought of it as their own language, separate from annoying noises. It'd just been... well, it'd just always been there.

"Oh, sorry, I was nerding out again, wasn't I? My siblings say I don't always have to go that deep."

For some reason a flash of irritation flooded through Nathan. Who said that? It made him want to fight them. "You weren't going too deep or anything like that. I... it makes sense. Uh, you make sense."

She flushed again, and if that wasn't prettier than the first time. "You think so?"

"Yeah, I know so."

A slow, sweet smile spread across her features and if she didn't practically light up. "Thanks, Nathan. I appreciate that. More than you know."

The moment hung heavy in the air between them, filled with a sort of tension that Nathan wasn't sure if he was imagining or not. Maybe it was just what normal conversation felt like, but he couldn't help but feel like it was something... *else.*

But the moment was gone when Clara cleared her throat. "Right. Well, why don't we get to the garden?"

He nodded, but as they walked along, he couldn't help but think that Clara was pretty good with humans too.

17

Clara

True to his word, Nathan seemed to be on his best behavior. He even smiled! Laughed! But as the minutes ticked by, Clara couldn't help but notice that with all of his anger simmered down a bit, there was a *whole* lot of something else simmering below his surface.

It was clear to her that the rage that had been so sharp against her was a shield, and underneath it was a very, very sad man who really loved his home. And perhaps if that was it, she wouldn't feel so strange, but there was something else there. Something she hadn't anticipated and didn't have a name for.

The best she could describe it was as some sort of intensity, one that made her feel his eyes on her even when she wasn't looking, one that felt like it was somewhere between expectation and terror, leaving her blood thrumming through her veins with a new sort of electricity.

Oh... actually, she probably should curb any talk or idioms about electricity while she was dealing with a man recovering from being hit by lightning.

"So, do you have a particular way you want this first set of seedlings planted?" she asked, kneeling as she was by his first garden bed.

Nathan nodded to her from the low, collapsible stool she'd snuck into his closet for him to use, then handed her the first tray.

"I'd like these to go in this area," he said calmly, lightly. Sometimes there was still a sharp, bitter edge to the words that left his mouth, but Clara understood that, in a way. He was trying, truly, but that didn't mean that it all was gone completely. Like she'd told Cass many times, it was the baby steps that mattered.

"Right, oooh, I see we have the cabbage here. What's the proper spacing on those again?"

She knew what it was. She knew almost every vegetable requirement for things in their area, a side effect from Papa's luscious garden. But she also knew that much of Nathan's anger came from him feeling inadequate and useless, so why not give him a way to help?

"You know what it is but thank you for trying."

Drat. The only issue was that Mr. Westbrook was clearly too smart for his own good. If she tried to softball him things to make him feel better, he'd only feel worse. *Pitied.* One thing Cass had made extremely clear during her recovery was that pity was like a clinging, oily sort of blanket that would wrap around her and smother any pride and motivation she had for the day. That certainly wasn't something Clara wanted to do to Nathan.

Not at all.

"I know for most of these, yeah, but every farmer has a preference, you know?"

"A preference on cabbage?"

There, the one corner of his lip she could see quirked up in the tiniest grin. He was bantering with her, that was good. It was too bad that he'd specifically angled himself so his more scarred side was facing away, but maybe that too could change in time.

Maybe. Baby steps, she had to remind herself. She wanted to get him to the point where he would feed himself regularly and not immediately lose all hope. It was a journey, that was for certain.

"Please, this is a homestead. You know that everyone has their rituals, processes and superstitions," Clara answered matter-of-factly. Nathan seemed to consider that a moment, then nodded.

"I suppose you're right. Fine then. I'll list out all the 'vegetable' preferences I have."

"Please and thank you!"

The conversation between them was starting to flow better. And even the silent moments were a comfortable silence, nonetheless. Whenever she finished a row of seedlings, she would move on to another and coax Nathan into giving her instructions, and sometimes those instructions would slide into anecdotes or stories. More often than not, Clara found herself telling a story about Papa or comparing Nathan's garden to her father's, but Mr. Westbrook didn't seem to mind.

"Wow, we're making great time, aren't we?" she asked when the cabbages, lettuce and carrots were all done.

"So far, but the spinach and beans can be a big time-soak."

"Is that so? Why's that?"

"Because they're particular, that's all. The runner beans gotta be by their stakes, and the spinach has to shade their roots when they're bigger. But you don't want to accidentally put bush beans where a runner or pole bean should be, because then that's taking a vital lattice spot that it doesn't need."

"Ahhh, I see. Beans were always Papa's thing. I was usually in charge of planting the squash and gourds."

"You always split up the planting the exact same way?"

"Some things yes, some things no, but beans were always Mama's thing. She grew different types from all over. Dragon tongue bush beans, scarlet runner beans, you name it. And after she died... well..."

To her surprise, Nathan nodded knowingly. "They're his thing now. A sort of connection."

A connection, yes. Exactly that, but still, so strange to hear it out of someone's mouth. "You've lost someone?"

"Haven't we all?"

Well, that was a huge non-answer.

"You just seemed to get it so fast. Maybe I'm just not used to talking to people outside my family, but usually people don't... they don't understand, I guess."

Nathan didn't reply to that at all, just leafing through the notebook she'd asked him to get. After several long moments and three planted sprouts, Clara gave up on him answering at all.

But then words did come out, low, so low. Almost a whisper. "My grandmother, when I was young."

"Your grammie?"

"Yeah. She was the glue that held my family together. My father, well, he was a drunken mistake and my mother, she had her demons. My grandmother helped her get clean, helped her raise me. We all lived together, until she passed."

"I'm sorry, Nathan."

Clara didn't know what to say, her heart opening up into one big ache. She couldn't imagine her life without her supportive father, the same as she couldn't imagine what it was like to have a mother who struggled with addiction.

"My mother was sober for twelve years thanks to my grandmother, but less than a year after she passed, my mom started using again." Nathan let out a dry sound. "You know, that's the catch twenty-two about getting clean that they don't tell you. You fight for years and years to resist your sickness, but when you slip up, your body can't handle what you used to do. That's why so many overdoses happen. Just people who've been fighting the good fight making a single mistake."

Clara swallowed, the picture painting itself easily in her mind. So much of the hurt that Nathan radiated made sense. And then... and then he was hit by lightning? That seemed awfully unfair.

"And from then on you were alone?"

"Not entirely. I had some cousins, some nice ladies from church, an uncle who came up from where he'd retired in Mexico. They were enough to get me through the worst part, help me finish my last year of high school, but after that, I was ready to move on. The town I was in, it had too many memories. Too many ghosts."

"Too many connections," Clara murmured quietly.

He nodded again. "Exactly. Too many connections."

He fell quiet, but Clara let him. She felt like a dozen or so significant puzzle pieces had been placed in her hands. So much of the mystery of Mr. Westbrook and why he was the way he was laid out before her in stunning technicolor.

But she could see the story was weighing heavily across his shoulders, and she knew it wasn't the time to push, prod or comment. Nathan just needed the quiet and time to come to terms with what he had said. When was the last time he'd ever opened up to someone enough to tell that story?

She didn't know, but it filled her with the hope that he trusted her with it, nonetheless.

It was hours later when Clara looked up from the first garden bed to see that the sun was beginning to set.

"Oh, my goodness. How long have we been out here?"

Nathan blinked then pulled his phone. "Wow, a little over four hours."

"Four hours?" Clara stood up only for her back to give a mighty twinge. "Oh, yup, that was definitely four hours. Geez, I'm too young to feel this old!"

Nathan gave her a sort of rueful look, and Clara flushed. Right, maybe she shouldn't complain about her lack of mobility in front of the guy fighting to get his body right after literal lightning shot through him.

"Right, so what about something to eat? Maybe I can whip up a quick dinner and we'll go our separate ways?"

"You don't have to stay for dinner. I'll just finish up with this planting. We still have all the potatoes slips to put in the ground."

Clara felt the frown coming on and yet she still couldn't stop it from tugging down at her features. "You're going to stay out here?"

"Yep. I need to get a bunch more done if we're going to stay on schedule. We're behind enough as it is."

"Oh, geez…" Clara didn't like the idea of him staying outside, all by his lonesome. What if he fell? What if another coyote showed up? What if he had a seizure? She didn't know if he had seizures, but she'd read that people who were recovering from lightning strikes could sometimes suffer from them.

"You know what, why don't I come by tomorrow and finish this up?"

"But tomorrow is Sunday."

He said it so matter of factly that it actually startled her. She figured that he had forgotten about their deal for him to go to church with her, and she wasn't going to press it until a week or so after planting.

"Yes."

"Don't you have church?"

"Don't *we* have church, you mean?" she said, testing the waters.

"I mean, yes, I know that's part of the deal, but I fail to see what that has to do with my garden being planted."

"It has to do with it because you and I are going to the early service, then I'll come back here, and we'll finish up stuff."

He let out a light chuckle, but it didn't feel mean. "You're gonna come to my little hovel dressed like you were on the first day?"

"Dressed like… *oh.*" Clara had forgotten about that. She really had shown up at his place for the first time in one of her pseudo vintage numbers and heels, hadn't she? Hah, it was a far cry from the overalls and work clothes she tended to wear around his place currently. "I'll make sure to bring a change of clothes."

"Sounds like a deal."

Clara looked down at his offered hand. He was wearing gloves, as usual, even though he hadn't touched the dirt at all.

Had she ever seen him without those? She didn't think so. Maybe that day when he was drunk as a skunk? Too bad she'd been so distracted by the situation that she hadn't noticed.

"Deal," Clara said, shaking his hand firmly.

And just like that, she had Sunday social plans.

18

Nathan

$\mathscr{H}$e was going to church.
　　　　Gross.

It wasn't that he didn't like the church. It had always been a nice place to go whenever he needed edifying or wanted some warmth and comfort. It reminded him of his grandmother and the services that she would always drag him and his mother to.

But ever since he'd been struck by lightning, he'd had a hard time finding that same comfort. It didn't help that he'd had to fight with his insurance for months, the corrupt company trying to deny him because it was an 'act of God.' Kind of hard not to hold a grudge when the Big Man in the Sky was being used as a reason to deny him care.

And Nathan had needed a lot of care.

There'd been the skin debriding, the skin grafts, the phys-ical therapy. There'd been further surgeries to repair things inside of him that he hadn't even known he had broken. It had all stacked on top of each other, and every time he had to call to fight the insurance agency, that grudge got bigger and bigger.

"Oh, there you are!"

Nathan looked up to the top of the church steps, the supposed wheelchair ramp they were building still being cobbled together. But the not-quite-ready ramp didn't hold his attention for longer than a blip, because there was Miss Clara Miller, standing in front of the church doors in all her Sunday glory.

Oh.

How had he never noticed her before? Sure, he usually went to the later services, but she did plenty of things in the church. The social lunches, the Bible studies. He'd heard plenty of her and yet he couldn't remember seeing her even once.

...maybe he just hadn't been paying attention to the right things.

"Glad to see you made it!" She grinned brightly, her ruby lips parting into a blinding smile.

"I'm a man of my word," he said, trying to steady his voice. How was it possible for one human to look so *bright*? From the blue heels she was wearing and the mint of her dress, to her auburn hair curled above her head, she practically glowed with... well, whatever it was that she had.

"Of course, I never doubted that. It's just, well, you know how health things are. Sometimes a bad day just happens."

A lot of people had told him various kind and under-standing things since he'd come back home, but Clara was one of the few he actually believed knew what she was talking about and meant exactly what she said.

"Fair enough."

"Right, anyway, shall we go in? It's early enough that all the best donuts and bagels aren't gone yet."

"You don't have to convince me twice."

Swallowing hard, Nathan walked up the stairs and back into a place that had once been a part of his heart and most certainly wasn't any longer.

It was uncomfortable, that was for certain. He could feel eyes on him as soon as he was in the doors, feel the whispers grate against his skin. It was uncomfortable, making his every nerve light up and his muscles tense. He couldn't escape the mental image of his own twisted face being pushed to the forefront of his mind, which made him feel cornered by it all.

He *hated* being cornered.

"Are you okay?" Clara asked him.

Nathan didn't answer right away, jerking back to the moment to realize that they were standing in front of the breakfast table.

"Um, yeah, I was just... distracted."

"Hmm." She didn't say anything else for a moment, her eyes looking over him like she could see through all his bluster and posturing to the scared and scarred man that he'd become. "Do you want a bagel?"

"What? Oh yeah, uh. Everything bagel, wouldn't mind it."

"Good choice! And cream cheese?"

"Salmon. Can't believe you actually have salmon flavored cream cheese in here."

"Yeah, well, it's too difficult to get lox and at least one little old lady will complain about the smell."

Nathan managed to huff a small laugh, but his heart just wasn't in it. He felt nauseous, and even nice, still-warm bagels with fancy cream cheese wasn't going to help that. He just wanted to crawl under his covers and sleep the day away. And maybe the next one too.

There was a bit of a clang in front of him, and he realized that Clara had set down the butterknife she was spreading with authority.

"Let's go."

"Huh?" Nathan blinked at her, wondering if he had missed out on a chunk of conversation.

"Let's go. Leave."

Clara began to stride out and Nathan found himself following her in bewilderment. "What? But the deal is—"

"I know what the deal is, but I also know that you're not ready. Church is meant to be a good thing, not stress you out. So, let's go."

"But... but..."

Suddenly, his hand was in hers, and he wished he could feel the softness of her skin through the gloves he always wore. "It's all about baby steps, okay? I appreciate that you tried, but the time's not quite right now."

"And... and you're not angry?"

She shook her head. "At least, not at you. I love this church, but I'm not blind to all the staring. And I know how rumors and gossip love to fly. I had hoped my family here would be better, but that will be a battle for a different day."

Huh.

She really was something.

Nathan nodded, his voice unable to work itself around the lump in his throat, and then she was gently pulling him out toward the main doors.

He could have gotten there himself. After all, it was the only church in town and the one that he'd attended for a couple years. But it was so much easier to let her guide him. All he had to do was focus on the sound of her voice and the click of her heels.

There were more whispers, more looks, but all of them started to fall away a little more every time Clara looked over her shoulder to check that he was just fine. She was like a shield, protecting him from the mocking deluge his own mind had no problem sinking into.

And then, just as suddenly as she'd grabbed his hand, they were outside, and he could breathe again.

"I'm sorry," he blurted out, hand over his chest as he tried to calm his thundering heart. What kind of man was he? Getting spooked from some old biddies and other church folk? Pathetic.

"What for?"

Nathan could only manage a shrug, his words escaping him.

"Look, Nathan, like I said, it's fine. There's nothing to apologize for, and you didn't do anything wrong. Let's just head to your place, reset, and plant the best fall garden you've ever had. How about that?"

Nathan nodded again, his tongue double thick within his mouth. Where did all of his words go?

"Are you safe to drive?"

Safe to drive? He hadn't been drinking. What did she—

As he puzzled it, a wave of dizziness passed over him, making him sway slightly on his feet. Suddenly he remembered how he and Clara had first met, with him laid out on his floor in misery.

Breath quickening, his chest began to feel tight. Too tight. It was like he couldn't draw in a full lungful, his skin tightening and tightening until he felt like he would just pop like a balloon.

"Nathan? Can you hear me?"

Someone was holding both of his hands. Who? Right. Clara. He knew that. He was standing with Clara in the church parking lot. He hadn't even made it to the service; the trip to the bagel table had apparently been too much for him.

But if he was in the church parking lot, why wasn't there any ground under his feet? He was falling. He was falling and he wasn't ever going to—

"Nathan, I think you're having a panic attack. My youngest sister Cici used to get these all the time. I need you to breathe with me, okay?"

Breathe? He couldn't breathe! That was the whole problem.

"Come on, I know it's hard, but just try to do what I do. Breathe in. Breathe out. Chest rising, chest falling."

Her voice was so soothing, beckoning him back to the world. Breathe in with her? Okay, he could try. Inhale. Exhale. He just followed her mantra until finally, his skin stopped tightening and his chest stopped collapsing on itself.

"There you go. You're doing great. Keep breathing. Now, in your head, I want you to notice five things you can see about this parking lot. You don't have to tell me. You just need to think about it."

Five things? Okay. He could do that. The blacktop was unreasonably hot considering the day wasn't that overheated. There were plenty of cars around him that were older than he was. And... was that a motorcycle? Huh. Who at the church owned a motorcycle?

"Yeah, I knew you could do it. Just keep breathing. Next, think of four things you can smell."

Bit by bit, he went through the list, following her voice. Three things he felt. Two things he could hear. And then, by the end of it, he was able to finally draw in a deep, steady breath.

"Hey, there's my friend, back again. You want to sit down in your truck?"

Nathan looked at Clara, *really* looked at her, and it was like she was glowing. Really, truly radiating light. Her round, heart face, her intense eyes in direct contrast with her soft, plush lips, she was truly beautiful, but most importantly, it felt she really, truly *saw* him.

And she was the first one who hadn't just seen the lightning bolt that had torn his life in two.

"Yeah, I do."

"Alright, you get in, and I'll drive you home."

"What about your car?"

"I'll have Charlie drive it to your place when we're done, and I'll take him back home later. That is, if you're comfortable with it, of course."

Nathan thought for a moment, but his brain seemed sluggish and thick. "Uh, yeah. Yeah, I think that's a good idea."

"Alright, can I have your keys? I'll go put mine in my glove compartment."

"Okay, yeah. Um, let me just fish 'em out."

Anywhere else, that would have been an awful idea. But their town was so small that no one could steal a car without it being noticed. Also, most people wouldn't ever *want* to steal a car.

Nathan handed his keys over and Clara took them, letting go of his hands to walk to her Jeep and put her keys in the glovebox. By the time she walked back, he was feeling a little more grounded.

"You wanna slide into the passenger seat?"

"Sure, yeah."

He wished her hands were still gripping his. He wished she

was still talking to him like he was the center of the world and wasn't crazy.

But the embarrassment was beginning to sink in, ebbing away the warm, comforting feeling that he'd sunken into. But he didn't want to let it. Instead, he sank his fingers into that beautiful feeling and wouldn't let it go. Not even that lurking darkness inside of him could rip that away.

"Do you know which way to go from here?"

"Yeah, I know the way. You just rest, okay? Do you want me to stop and get some soda?"

"Yeah, actually. A soda sounds nice."

Clara nodded and then they were driving off. It wasn't a long trip back to his place, even with a stop at one of the two gas stations around to grab some cold sodas, but it was long enough to let him feel a little less like his world was going to shake apart.

"Thank you, you know."

"For what?" Clara murmured as they pulled onto the final road that led to his little homestead.

For what? How could she not know? "For, you know, everything."

"It's nothing. Just being a good neighbor."

Nathan nodded, unsure what to do with the knot of emotions deep within his chest. He suddenly felt like he was being overwhelmed with a deluge of feelings, but he hadn't anticipated most of them and couldn't untangle them all.

But that was okay. Maybe he didn't have to untangle them at the moment. Maybe he could just be content with the moment and the fact that he could breathe again.

Maybe.

Finally, Clara pulled up, turning his truck off in her usual spot. Funny that she had a 'usual' spot. But it was true. During the week that she'd been gone, that spot had sat empty like a beacon reminding him of everything he'd done wrong to drive her away.

"You want to go in and rest for a minute? We can take the rest of the day off if you want. I can always change my schedule around and come by tomorrow."

Nathan thought for a moment. Sure, it was tempting to just go inside and collapse on his couch with a cold beer and try to forget the wreck he'd become, but he was serious when he'd promised himself that he was tired of moping. He was going to be proactive and do the things that he loved.

"How about we drink our drinks, then get to finishing the garden?"

"Sure. I'd like that."

19

Clara

"I'll brew you some tea."

"Hmm?" Clara blinked, not realizing that she'd been staring at Nathan out of the corner of her eye.

She'd been so certain that he was going to be furious that she'd pushed him too hard, but instead... he seemed almost peaceful?

Maybe he was in shock, maybe the explosion was going to come later. She had no idea; she just felt a bit on edge, waiting for the inevitable.

But the important thing was that she'd been there for him —even if she was the one who had kind of put him in that situation. She'd just thought that church would have been so good for him, to see familiar faces and get out of his rut.

She'd pushed too hard. She'd put her needs ahead of his own, and that was the worst way to help him. In fact, it wasn't helping him at all. It was selfish. She thought she'd learned with Cass that the needs of the hurt superseded the needs of everyone else.

"Earl Grey, right?"

She blinked again and suddenly Nathan was handing her a steaming cup of tea. "Oh yes, thank you. How did you know?"

Nathan gave her a soft look, one that she'd never seen on him before. "You never drank coffee and always brewed yourself tea. It's probably not as good as whatever you made, but I figure it's better than my dirty bean juice."

She couldn't help the lightest of chuckles. "I don't know that my dirty leaf juice is that much fancier."

"Seems that way to me."

There was something different about him, something she couldn't quite put her finger on. Maybe he was just hazy from his panic attack. Ugh, that had been something, that was for certain.

She couldn't get the image out of her head so it joined the many other images she had in her head of Mr. Westbrook. Him lying on the floor. Him passed out drunk on his couch. Him sitting on his stool, the sun just beginning to set behind him, highlighting the features he tried so hard to hide. Him standing, grinning and naming his chickens for her with a sort of tenderness to his words that only came from someone who respected and took care of their livestock.

What was it about Nathan that made him shine like a beacon to her? Was it the tragedy? Was it her need to take care of people? She always thought that she was never like Charity, but... she was beginning to doubt that.

"Does... does it smell off?"

For the third time, Clara blinked herself back to reality. Gosh, he had to think she was daft. She was just staring at the tea like it was going to talk to her, locked into her own thoughts. "Oh no, I just wanted it to cool down a little. Thank you. I can't believe you noticed such a thing."

"Believe it or not, I am somewhat cognizant of my surroundings."

Clara flushed and sipped at her tea. It wasn't one of Papa's brews, or her own, but it wasn't some generic brand either. Had he bought it just for her?

That thought made her chest constrict and her cheeks heat. Which was probably weird, and yet...

"It's good, thank you."

"No problem. How about we sit on my porch and finish our drinks?"

"Oh, did you make yourself something?"

He lifted the soda that she'd stopped and bought for him.

"Right, right. I knew that."

He nodded and gestured to the door. Clara didn't know why her body suddenly felt like it was ten minutes behind her brain, but she stuttered a bit before following him out.

There weren't any seats on his porch, so she stood there a moment in the doorway, looking like a complete dork. She was reminded of high school, when she never knew what to do with herself and her body just took up so much *space.*

But then Nathan shakily sat down on the steps leading up to his place and she followed suit, parking a respectable distance away from him, but hopefully not an unsociable one.

Why was she so nervous? She didn't know. She wanted to blame her sweating palms on the hot tea in her hands, but she knew that wasn't it. So, what was it? Why did she suddenly feel so unsure of someone she'd been so comfortable with before?

Was it the panic attack? She'd experienced it dozens and dozens of times with Cici. After Mama had passed, she'd had the worst night terrors and had to take nearly a year-long break from school. Panic attacks had hit her nearly weekly, and even the smallest things would set her off. It'd taken a lot of therapy, love, and just continuing to live on for her to get a handle on them, and the entire family had learned a lot of ways to support her.

So no, it wasn't the panic attack. But it also absolutely was the panic attack. The world had shifted between them yet again, and she didn't know where her feet were supposed to be.

They sat there in silence, just drinking their drinks, until she got to the bottom of her cup and it was suddenly all too much. Jumping to her feet, she did a good stretch, popping her back.

"Well, I guess I better go change."

Nathan didn't say anything, just gave her a quiet nod, but she took that as her cue. She grabbed the backpack she'd brought and hurried up to his bathroom.

Once she had that door closed between them, it was like she could take a solid breath.

"Calm down, Clara. What's wrong with you?"

She felt her cheeks with the back of her hands, and they were practically burning. Goodness, she needed to get it together. She couldn't even really name the fluttering in her belly or the quickening in her veins. The closest thing she could compare it to was in the *African Queen* when they were going down choppy water that their boat couldn't possibly survive.

"Just get changed and go out there. You're acting like a crazy-head and Nathan is relying on you!"

Her self-lecture didn't really help, but she still shimmied into her work clothes, shoved her nicer ones away and rushed down the stairs. Nathan was in the kitchen, putting his bottle in the recycling bin she'd gotten him.

"You ready?"

"Yeah. Let's get those seedlings planted."

He just nodded again, and she would have thought his wordlessness was because he was angry at her if it weren't for the soft, subtle smile he sent her.

Goodness, since when did he look at her like that?

Since when did *anyone* look at her like that?

Thankfully she didn't have to answer that, and they walked over to the part of the plot they still needed to get to. But just when Clara knelt down and Nathan sat on his stool, a truly violent crack of thunder sounded above, and a drenching rain was suddenly pouring down.

"Oh, criminy! What are the chances? Nathan, would you—"

Then it happened. In retrospect, it should have been obvious; Clara knew what always accompanied thunder, but when the sky lit up with a blinding bolt of lightning a few miles away, everything went haywire.

"Oh, wow. That was a big one, wasn't it?" She turned to Nathan on his stool, her words hitting her as she did. Did she just refer to a bolt of lightning as a 'big one' to a man who had *recently been struck by lightning?* Clara had done a lot of clueless things in her life, but she was pretty sure that was going to take the cake. "I'm sorry about that, Nathan. I wasn't thinking. You want to head in?"

It was so hard to see him, even just from a few feet away. The rain was falling in thick sheets, and she was fairly certain that at least a few of their planted seedlings were going to get washed away in the deluge. But the seeds didn't matter. She wasn't sure what the chances were of being struck by lightning twice in one lifetime, but she didn't want to find out.

"Nathan?"

Finally, when she was almost on top of him, she finally saw him, sitting there on his stool and staring up at the sky.

"Nathan?"

Maybe it was just the thick cloud cover, maybe it was the almost literal wall of water between them, but the man looked almost gray, frozen stock-still like a statue.

"NATHAN! Come on. We need to go inside!"

He didn't answer and what little color he had before drained from him even more. What was Clara supposed to do? She needed to think. *Think.*

Hadn't... hadn't she talked to someone about something like this? It was a while ago, but she felt like it was pulling at the edge of her memory. Something about a... a fugue state?

Oh! Yes! It had come up in a conversation with Missy when she was telling how she came into the family. She'd helped Bart when she'd first met him and gotten him back home when he was wandering around outside barefoot. What had she said she'd done?

"Um... um... soothing? Calm, direct, small words? That couldn't have been all of it." Clara swallowed hard when another booming crack of thunder sounded up ahead. "Right, time is of the essence. Nathan. Nathan, can you hear me?"

Instead of answering, he started to sway backwards. It was like he was completely stuck, frozen by time and the lightning above. Clara couldn't help but feel awful for him. Poor guy had a panic attack, in addition to whatever was happening at the moment, all in one day.

"Nathan, remember the breathing exercise in the parking lot? Can you do that for me?"

He didn't even blink. Well, that wasn't working.

Clara felt a pulse of urgency up her spine. She *needed* to get him inside where there was no lightning. No thunder. Besides, she was sure with all his surgeries and recovery that he didn't need to be out in the open getting rained on.

"Nathan, I know I don't exactly have your permission, but if you don't answer me, I'm... well, I'm going to have to touch you. So, I *need* you to answer me, alright?"

He actually managed to blink, so that was an improvement, and his eyes focused on her like she was actually there. Clara's heart swelled, but then the whole sky was illuminated by another bolt of lightning. Nathan went right back to ghostly gray and unresponsive.

"Please, dear Lord on High, help me make the right decision," Clara muttered to herself before crouching by Nathan. "Alright, Mr. Westbrook, here goes nothing."

Gripping his waist, she pulled him forward, tilting him over her shoulder and then using all of the strength in her thighs to push herself up.

It took some doing, but she managed to fully stand, with Nathan slung over her shoulder. He didn't move, didn't react, but he sure did weigh quite a lot. Not as much as a homesteader of his stature should have, that was for certain, but he wasn't exactly a featherweight.

"Alright, Mr. Westbrook. Let's get you inside."

It wasn't exactly quick going, and once the wind started up, the rain went sideways, and it was even harder to see. But Clara trusted her footing, moving carefully bit by bit until she hit something solid. The porch stairs! Excellent. Just a few more steps and she would be under the awning.

Back aching, thighs burning, Clara willed herself up the first step. Then the second. Then the third and she was finally out of the worst of the deluge. Granted, there was still plenty of dampness considering just how tilted the rain was, but it was much better than before.

"Almost there, Mr. Westbrook. I hope you don't mind that we're going to make your couch pretty wet."

He didn't answer, just let out a low groan, but that was better than nothing, so she kept on going. The door wasn't exactly easy, but one strong shoulder was able to pop it open and then she was inside. Her muscles were screaming—she hadn't even warmed up, after all—but she made herself keep going.

Finally, she made it—and practically threw Nathan on the couch. Sure, it wasn't exactly the most dignified way to let him down, but her back was incredibly irritated at her and she wasn't sure that it was going to last a moment longer. But something about his back hitting the couch must have somehow grounded him, because Nathan blinked again.

"C-Clara?"

"There's a storm out there, Mr. Westbrook, and you're having a bad reaction. Is there anything I can do to help?"

"Uh... Meds. Upstairs."

"You have meds for this? What do they look like? Do you know the name?"

There was another truly awful crack of thunder outside, and once more, he didn't answer, staring up at the ceiling like he was watching the lightning play across the white surface.

"Nathan? You have meds for this. I need to know what they look like or what they're called."

"White pills. Right-hand side of the cabinet."

"Okay, I'll get those for you."

She wished that she had a name. She wished she had a description of what the pills looked like beyond just their color.

White wasn't exactly a plethora of adjectives. But she couldn't just sit there, not when he had something that would help him.

So up the stairs Clara went, leaving very wet and muddy footprints in her wake. Oh well. She would mop those up later. Considering how bad the storm was, Charlie certainly wasn't going to be delivering her Jeep anytime soon. But she was definitely going to need to text him.

"Thank you again, Charity, for that waterproof phone case," Clara murmured, practically erupting into the upstairs bathroom. Sliding a bit, she caught herself on the rug and flung the medicine cabinet open.

"Oh, that is a *lot* of bottles..."

Well, he'd said right side, so at least that eliminated over half of them. Grabbing five off the shelf, she popped off the tops one by one and peeked inside. Blue pill. Blueish pill. Yellowish pill.

"Ah! White pill!" There it was, an oblong shape sitting at the bottom of the bottle. But just to be sure, she popped open the next bottle and saw there was a white, hexagon pill in the bottom of that too. "Oh... drat."

She'd just have to take both of them. But wait... she didn't check the right half of the top shelf!

"Ugh, I need to calm down. I'm being careless." And she didn't know why. After everything with her mother, everything with Cass, she'd gotten used to maintaining plenty of calm in dire situations. But her hands were shaking, she was wet all the way through to her underthings, and her whole body was *very* angry at her sudden heavy lifting.

Taking a deep breath, she cleared the four or so bottles and popped the lids off those too. Sure, she was making an awful mess, but that could also be cleared up later.

"Come on, come on..."

Sure enough, there was a third bottle with white pills, but only a third bottle. It was better than nothing, so Clara raced down the stairs.

Nathan was sitting up at least, but his face was still an alarming shade of gray. A foul order hit her nose and she realized he'd gotten sick on the floor in front of him.

Oh, dear. Definitely not good.

"Nathan, there are three white pills. Do you know which you need?"

He held out his hand, which was much more promising than she'd expected, and she placed all three bottles in his palm. He wasn't going to take all three, was he?

Clara watched, anticipation coursing through her, followed quickly by relief when he looked in all three and just took two of the oblong ones.

"Those for panic attacks?" she blurted as he dry swallowed them. But Nate just shook his head, not answering as he sat back against the couch and stared at the wall. "Right. I'm going to get you some water. Maybe some food." Yeah, there was almost nothing that carbs and protein couldn't solve.

When she returned, she was glad that he slowly drank from the water bottle she got him and nibbled at the mixed nuts she'd grabbed from his cabinet. It was slow going, but eventually, the color started to return to his cheeks, although he still flinched every time the thunder boomed or lightning flashed.

"It's for PTSD."

"Hmm?"

"The pills. They help with the flight or fight response. All that adrenaline."

"Oh." Goodness, she'd asked that question nearly an hour earlier. "But you didn't fight or flight."

"No. I froze. That's what I do. I just freeze. Doctor says it's a thing."

"Oh, should I call the doctor?" Why hadn't she thought of that earlier? Alejandro was dating her sister, for goodness sake.

"Probably smart."

"Right, I'll go do that."

Clara headed into the kitchen where she'd left her very soggy phone case during her snack hunt and shook it out. Just like Charity had promised, none of it actually managed to get inside to her phone, but the outer layer of the thing needed a good wipe off. Luckily, after that, it was a quick button press and Alejandro's line was ringing.

"Clara, what's going on? Is Cassidy alright?"

"Oh yeah, she's fine. I mean, actually, I don't know. I'm not with her right now."

"You're not at the ranch? There's a severe storm going on right now, Clara!"

"I know. It kind of caught me while I was out. I'm actually with another one of your patients, Mr. Westbrook."

"Nathan? Is he alright?"

"The storms not doing him too well. He froze up, as he puts it. I got him talking now and got him his medicine, but can you come see him?"

"Clara, I don't think you understand how bad the storm is outside. There's a severe thunderstorm warning. No one is supposed to be traveling. If he was in dire straits, I might risk it, but if you have him up and talking, the best thing to do is comfort him, distract him and get him some good calories in."

"Okay, I can do that."

"Oh, and Clara, call me if anything else happens or he seems to get worse, okay?"

"Will do."

"I'm sorry you're stuck in this, but if anyone can handle it, it's you. I'm glad Nathan has someone like you by his side."

Someone like me? "Thanks, Alejandro. I'll do my best."

"You always do."

With another goodbye, he hung up, leaving Clara alone in Nathan's kitchen. Setting her phone back down, she took a deep breath.

"Good calories. I can do that."

Yes, that was a good place to start.

20

Nathan

*E*verything was hazy.

Sometimes Nathan knew exactly where he was and that he was making a right fool of himself for the second time in one day. But sometimes he'd slip off to another time, like when he was first struck by lightning, or the time he'd been knocked over by a very angry sow when he'd first started home-steading on his own.

What had Dr. Lumis called it? Disassociating? That sounded right. Yeah, he was disassociating. Had he taken his meds that were supposed to help with all that adrenaline? He couldn't remember. He...

"Hey, I made you a nice ham sandwich, extra meat, extra cheese, and extra pickle slices. I think I read somewhere about the brine in it being a quick way to get some electrolytes. Oh! And also, this sports drink from the case I dropped off last time

I went grocery shopping for you. It's room temperature, but I figured that would be alright."

Who was that?

Blinking for several long minutes, Nathan felt himself drift into his own body, and he looked up to see Clara leaning over him with a tray in her hands. Where did she even get that tray from? Had she brought it?

"Clara?" he heard himself ask. His voice sounded so strange, like tin in his ears.

"Hey there, friend. Is that medicine kicking in?"

He didn't answer right away, trying to figure out if it had. Time was beginning to make more sense and he was much less floaty than he'd been before. But then there was an explosion right outside his window, and he jolted right back out of himself.

He was back in high school, diving into the pool that his swim team practiced in, water rushing past him. It was peaceful, for just a moment, and then he was putting his everything into making sure he could swim as fast as possible to the other side.

He was fifteen, shoveling the drive as his grandmother stood in the door with a coffee mug in her hands.

He was a young man, standing over an open grave as his mother was lowered into the earth.

He was... he was...

"Hey, you wanna take a big bite for me?"

"Huh?"

Oh. He was thirty years old and having a PTSD episode in his living room, and a beautiful woman was trying to feed him.

Yeah, that made sense.

But there Clara was, looking at him with those kind yet

intense eyes of hers. "I cut it in diagonals, figured it would make it easier to chew."

Nodding, Nathan shakily reached for the sandwich then brought it to his mouth. Everything seemed so mechanical, like he was one step behind his own experience. But then the salty, savory warmth hit his tongue and it was a little easier to tie himself back to the world.

Suddenly he was ravenously hungry, like painfully so, and he was biting into the sandwich with gusto.

"Ah, there you go! Glad you like it." Clara sounded far too happy for him just eating a sandwich, but he didn't stop until it was gone, and then she was immediately handing him a drink. He gulped that down too, and the world cleared out even more.

"Are you back with me, Mr. Westbrook?"

Nathan frowned, his stomach churning which wasn't exactly a good thing with all the food and drink he'd just crammed down. "I think we're at the point you can call me Nathan. There's never really been a Mr. Westbrook."

"Alright then, *Nathan*. It's good to see you back. You still hungry?"

"No, I... I think I'm alright." There was that embarrassment boiling up inside of him, making him want to sink into the couch and never return. "I'm sorry for everything. If you want to, uh, go home, I can handle things from here."

"Are you kidding? I'm not leaving you alone after the day you've had! This is one for the records, really."

And there was that kindness and understanding of hers, which only made him feel worse. All the exhaustion and tension surged up on him and before he knew it, he was snapping again.

"I don't need any charity!"

"Again, not Charity. That's my sister." She straightened, and the cool expression she fixed on her face made Nathan feel even worse.

Hadn't he promised that he wouldn't snap at her anymore?

"Anyway, there's an awful storm outside and I literally can't leave. I'm sorry, Mr. We— *Nathan,* but I'm stuck here."

"The storm?" Oh right. That was the whole reason he'd blanked out, hadn't he? He should remember that. "It's that bad?"

"High winds and severe lightning. So, if you don't mind, let's skip all this unpleasant business and settle in for an evening and possibly a full night together."

"Spending the night?"

He shouldn't have said it like that; he sounded like some virginal schoolboy. But he was used to small-town, Christian life, and an unwed woman spending the night at a bachelor's house was certain to cause gossip. Especially if that woman was a rich heiress from a famous ranching family.

"Unless you have a magical teleporting ability you didn't tell me about, absolutely."

Nathan swallowed harshly; the thunder suddenly seemed much less important outside. "Oh... okay. Um, should I make you dinner?"

She laughed gently, and that sound made him feel somewhat better. "I have it handled. You know what, why don't you rest and maybe play some games on your phone or play some music?"

"I can do that."

She nodded and walked out of the room, her wet shoes making little squeaking sounds as she went. But it wasn't until she was gone that he realized that he was utterly soaked too.

Well, that was entirely uncomfortable.

It took some effort, but he worked his way to his feet. His

body still felt strangely detached, but he felt mostly steady. Until a crack of thunder sounded again and lightning illuminated his entire house.

Suddenly his body was across the room, halfway under an end table, and he realized that he'd dove for cover. Why had he done that? He was inside, and he'd made sure that he had a lightning rod for safety on his property ever since the accident.

...maybe he should start seeing his therapist more regularly again.

But first, a nice warm shower and dry clothes. And, judging by how heavy his limbs felt, maybe he could pass out on his bed and let his meds do their job.

Yeah, that sounded like a good idea. And maybe that would also allow him to procrastinate about thinking on how Clara Miller was apparently going to be staying in his dinky little bachelor's cabin overnight.

Although he didn't even think the hottest shower could distract him from that.

WHEN NATHAN WOKE UP, he felt like he'd been hit by a truck. A truck with a particularly malicious vendetta against him.

Groaning, he pushed himself up and realized he was in his bed. Foggily, he remembered getting out of the shower and barely drying off before flinging himself under the covers. He'd still been pretty messed up, but it seemed his nap had done him good.

Then again, was it a nap, or a sleep?

Glancing out the window, he saw that the rain was still going as hard as ever and... was that hail? That definitely looked like hail. It did seem to be dark out, but he couldn't tell if that was the same as when the storm started or if it had gotten worse.

Where was his phone?

Oh right, he'd left it in his very wet pants in his bathroom. That definitely needed to be stuck in a bag of rice as soon as possible.

Grumbling to himself, Nate wiggled out of bed and put some thick, flannel pants over his boxers and threw on a T-shirt. Heading into his bathroom, he found it right where he thought it was and headed to his kitchen to find that bag of rice he was pretty sure that Clara had brought him.

It was really a credit to all the carrots he liked to eat that he didn't realize none of the lights in the house were on until he got to the bottom of the stairs. Or maybe it was just that he was still a bit out of it.

He preferred to think that it was the former, however.

Eyes already adjusted to the dark, he headed around the corner and into his kitchen only to find Clara there, candles lit all around her as she cooked on his gas range. What... what was she doing there?

A thundering boom outside shook the house yet again and everything came rushing back to him. Right, there was a severe storm and he'd freaked out. He hadn't done that in a while, but he guessed being outside, plus the incident at the church, had kind of put him into a bad spot.

How humiliating.

"Oh, hey there. How are you feeling?"

Clara turned to him, a smile across her pleasant features, and yet that kind grin wasn't what his eyes went to. No, instead they went straight to what she was wearing.

Gone were her church clothes. Gone were the overalls she'd

been wearing. No, she was in a pair of tight, black leggings he'd never seen her in before and one of his shirts.

Oh.

He knew his staring was obvious when she flushed and ran a hand over the buttons. "I hope you don't mind. I brought another pair of pants, but I realized I was out of tops. And I was just absolutely soaked. I went in and grabbed it while you were sleeping."

Nathan didn't know what to say. He wasn't mad—of *course* he wasn't mad—but he couldn't exactly say he was unaffected either. No, there was something *very* affecting about seeing Clara in his shirt, the ends of it almost down to the middle of her thighs and some of the buttons straining from the curves she had that he didn't.

It was so utterly domestic that, for a moment, he felt like he'd been transported into a different timeline. One where he was a normal guy with a normal family with a beautiful wife who cooked him a meal after a nice nap.

...what could have been.

"My clothes are probably dry if you want me to change. I can wash it!"

"No!" he said, probably a little too forcefully. But he very much didn't want Clara to change. The idea that she was in his home, in his clothes, filled him with a certain kind of pride he hadn't felt in so long. Almost like he was providing for her.

Almost like he was a real man again.

"It's fine. It's no big deal." He cleared his throat, looking for some sort of segue. "What are you making?"

"Oh, nothing too special. But I noticed you still had some pork chops in your freezer from my last grocery run, so I decided to grill that up with some Brussel sprouts and red potatoes."

"Nothing special, huh? If it requires more than two ingredients, it's special to me."

She laughed and it was like his mood lifted in time with each peal. Did she have a special power or was he just that pathetic? "That's a pretty low bar, my friend."

"What can I say? I like things simple."

"And what about homesteading is simple?"

"You... may have a point there. Why do everything in one step when you can do it in ten?"

She laughed again, only louder. Or did the storm abruptly get quieter? Honestly, Nathan wouldn't blame God for hushing the maelstrom just to listen to Clara be happy. It was easy to forget about all the mess in the world whenever she smiled like that.

Easy to forget about all the mess inside of him.

"You know I have a backup generator, right? Staple of every homestead."

She flushed at that, her cheeks turning a pretty pink once again. He missed that look, and seeing her wear it while half in his clothing?

God was being either incredibly thoughtful or incredibly malicious. The jury was still out.

"I figured, but I didn't really know where it was, and I didn't want to go outside in all of the mess. You know, since I already stole one of your shirts. Figured you didn't want me going through your entire wardrobe."

She could go through his whole dresser, his whole closet, heck, she could go through his old sports jersey locked in a trunk somewhere if it meant he could see her parade around in things that smelled like him. That *were* his.

"It's actually in my basement. I'll go turn it on and we can blow out these fire hazards."

"Sounds like a plan," she said, grinning again, the corners of her eyes crinkling. "Come back quick. This is almost all done."

Nate nodded, his heart thundering in his chest, but in a way that felt a lot less lethal than how it had in the parking lot. Was this really his life? Had he gone from falling apart in a parking lot and freezing like a rabbit in his own yard to having a beautiful, multimillionaire woman cooking him dinner in his kitchen while wearing his shirt?

Seemed like quite the transition. Maybe he was still asleep and all of it was a dream. Well, if it was, he certainly didn't want to wake up.

For being a dream, it certainly was still just as annoying to get his spare generator up and running. It wouldn't power his whole house, but it could handle some of the lights and his TV. Maybe even his DVD player if he was lucky.

Once it was done, he headed right back up the stairs just in time to see Clara plating the food, still grinning.

"Let me see if I can flip on the emergency lights in here." With a held breath, he found the one switch he'd hooked up to the generator's power supply and, sure enough, some weak lights flickered to life.

"Fantastic! Do you want to eat in the living room?"

"Sure. We can watch a movie, if you want."

He didn't know what made him say that. He hadn't even checked to make sure his TV would work. But the way Clara absolutely lit up made him happy that he had jumped the gun.

"Really? You think you have enough energy to stream something?"

"Oh, not streaming. DVD."

She let out a huff of a laugh. "Really? DVDs?"

"Yeah. Call me old-fashioned."

"Huh, okay. Well, will you grab a couple of water bottles while I take these plates in?"

"Of course."

He grabbed a couple from the fridge and followed after her, trying not to focus too much on her leggings. Hard to do, considering how her strong, assured stride made her wide hips sway a certain kind of way. But more than anything, he wanted to respect Clara, who had gone above and beyond in every way possible, so he kept his eyes firmly on the back of her head.

...well, mostly. He was only human, after all, and he appreciated God's beautiful work as much as the next person.

He was saved from his temptation when she set the plates on his coffee table and stood, wiping her hands on her pants. "So, where are these ancient discs of yours?"

"My DVDs?" he asked, setting the bottles down beside them. "Right over there, bottom three shelves of my bookcase."

He watched as her gaze flicked over to the tall case and then she practically flounced over to it. Funny, he'd never seen her move with such levity. Was this a side of Clara he never got to see? One when she wasn't in church or rescue mode? It made him wonder just how much he didn't know about the woman who so influenced his life.

She settled down on her knees, and Nathan couldn't help the quick flash of uncertainty that she might judge him for his collection choices. He knew he had eclectic tastes, but he also didn't like spending more than ten dollars on a DVD.

It turned out he didn't have much to worry about, because less than a minute in, Clara squealed in delight.

"You have *Some Like It Hot!?*"

Nathan flinched at first, the octave she had hit being about ten times higher than her normal volume. But after shaking his head for a moment, his brain caught up with what she had said.

"Yeah. I, uh, I like the classics."

Actually, his *grandmother* had liked the classics. He remembered watching tons of black and white movies while on the couch with her and his mother. They were wonderful memories, and every time he watched them, it was almost like he was back there with them.

"Oh my gosh. It's been ages since I watched this with anyone! Can we do this one, please? *Please*?"

There was no way on earth he could ever refuse that, not that he wanted to.

"Of course. I'll put it in and boot it up."

She let out another squeal, jumping to her feet and clapping her hands. A shake of the leg later, the movie menu was playing on loop.

"You want subtitles, or no?"

"Oh, subtitles, please. It makes it easier to catch things if I'm laughing or whatever."

"You seem really excited for this."

"Of course, I am! It's one of my favorites ever!"

"Really? You like classic movies?"

"Oh yes, I do. I've pretty much driven my family insane with watching these over and over again. Back before the DVD era, I wore out three different VHS machines."

"Really? Which ones?"

"*African Queen, It's a Wonderful Life* and *Rio Lobo*."

"*Rio Lobo*? You watch John Wayne?"

"I do. Some films I like better than others. I know there are some of his movies that *really* misrepresent Natives, but there's still some magic in the better ones."

Nathan mulled that over for a moment. He wasn't exactly used to people mentioning anything about Natives in classic cinema. "Are you an Indian?"

"No. But my cousin married one and she's taught me a lot. Besides, plenty of our own has Native and Latinx people, so I figure it's wise to understand the history of the place we live. You know, honor it."

"Hmm. I never thought of it that way."

"I know. It's mostly because our schooling system *really* doesn't like discussing it. Anyway, press play?"

"Right. Press play."

He did just that and the movie began, opening up in brilliant black and white. Clara clapped her hands yet again, settling back on the couch with her plate in her lap. Nathan tried to settle in too, but he had a feeling his eyes were going to be on the woman beside him rather than the film.

21

Clara

Watching *Some Like It Hot* was like slipping into a warm, comfortable bath after a long, stressful day. Clara knew she was mouthing the words to some scenes, but Nathan didn't complain. Heck, he even seemed interested when she blurted out trivia. Like how Marilyn Monroe was pregnant during some of the shooting and the scene where she kept forgetting her lines, so she had to read them off a chalkboard that the director wrote them on for her.

It was wonderful, a pleasant trip down memory lane, and she found her heart aching in that special, bittersweet way it did every time she watched one of her favorite love stories. Was it jealousy? Probably a little. She wished that she could be looked at like those leading men looked at their leading ladies. She wished that she lived in a time of gentleman and dances in ballrooms. She wished... she wished for so much, and none of it was possible.

"And here I was worried you'd think my tastes were outdated."

"Hardly," she answered, chuckling slightly. In fact, she'd been shocked to even see that he'd had it. Almost no one she knew cared about any movie that wasn't in color. And sure, old movies had racism, misogyny, and plenty of awful things in them, and she'd seen some films that really made her shudder. But there was still plenty of gems and magic, and she had memorized a good list of the best of those. "At least not to me. I love the style of old movies. The fashion of it, the music."

"The spectacle is pretty nice, isn't it? Movies seem to be mostly about explosions nowadays."

"Yeah, that does seem to be the trend." Clara let out a heavy sigh. "I wish there were dances as a social thing."

She'd meant to mutter that last part, but it came out a bit louder than that. Nathan cleared his throat—he seemed to do that a lot—then set his empty plate on the coffee table. She felt that small, pleasant warmth she always got whenever someone finished her food.

"Oh, you're a dancer? That on top of being super woman?"

"Super woman?" Clara laughed. Was he teasing her? His tone was genuine, but obviously he didn't think that of her. She wasn't superhero material. Especially not if it involved shoving her body into those spandex suits they tended to wear in the comics her cousin adored. "Hardly. I just, you know..." She trailed off, feeling the dreamy lilt of yesteryear float over her. "It would be nice to go to some event, have everyone freeze because I've entered with the most beautiful dress they've ever seen."

She heaved a sigh, lost in the daydream she'd sunken into

more times than she'd counted. "All eyes on me, most shocked, some admiring, everyone wondering who I am. I'm... ethereal, and for a moment no one approaches me because it's clear I'm not really meant to be a part of their world."

"Sounds lonely," Nathan murmured.

"But it's not. Because after a moment, some gentleman in a sharp suit and a dashing grin approaches me, offers me his hand. The big band starts up and then we float across the room. And then we're *both* not a part of their world. We're a part of our own. Just us, and the magic."

"You know, I've been to plenty of dances, and none of them have ever been anywhere near what I'd describe as magic."

Clara sighed again, her mood deflating slightly. "I wouldn't know."

He didn't answer right away, and her eyes flicked to him, expecting judgment from her. But instead he just looked shocked. "What do you mean, you wouldn't know?"

"I mean that no one has ever asked me to dance."

"Not even at school dances?"

"No. Not even then. Nobody wanted to dance with the fat girl who was five inches taller than them in heels."

His expression went stormy for a moment, and Clara worried she'd said something wrong. Hastily, she stood to grab the dishes so she could wash them, when she heard old music playing.

"Huh?"

She stood there a moment, wondering if she was having a stroke, before realizing that Nathan was playing the music from the slow dance scene in *Some Like It Hot* from his phone.

"What are you doing?"

To her great surprise, he stood up too and offered her his

outstretched hand. "Miss Clara Miller, would you dance with me?"

She looked at his hand, for once free of his gloves, and she saw the mottled pink and red skin there. She looked up at his face and those serious eyes of his. Then back to his outstretched hand.

"You're joking," she said with a nervous giggle, her chest crumpling slightly. She'd been jokingly asked out as pranks more time than she could count, and it still felt oh so crushing to be led on.

"No, ma'am. I'm not. Everyone should get to have at least one dance." Nathan faltered slightly, and she saw so much pain travel across his face as well. "Although I understand if you don't want it to be me—"

"No! I'd love to. It would be... nice."

"Alright then. I'll restart the song."

Clara stared at his hand a bit more before sliding her palm over his. His skin was an interesting texture, smooth in some places, rough in others, some too hot and some too cool. She wanted to look at his palm, study it, but she had a feeling that would cause Nathan to recoil.

And that was the last thing that she wanted. Something had shifted between them yet again, and Nathan was more open to her than he'd ever been.

"Thank you," he murmured as she rested her other hand on his shoulder and closed the last of the space between them. Her front was almost brushing against his, right where the button of his shirt was straining. She was going to need to reinforce that once she changed back into her own clothes.

"For what?" she whispered back, heart thundering in her ears. The music was just beginning to swell, and Nathan took the first step, guiding her backwards.

"For everything. For coming back. For helping me today. You're a saint, you know that?"

She felt her cheeks heat and shook her head. "Pffft. I wouldn't say that. I have the time, so why not do something productive with it?"

"It's more than that, though. You only had to drop off groceries and now you're helping me plant my garden and feed my animals."

Clara didn't know what to say to that. She was rich, so it just made sense that she could do more than the average person. That was all.

"I'm just helping however I can."

Nathan made an agreeable sound but didn't argue further, and they fell into the rhythm of it. Two steps backwards, three steps forward. One to the side. One to the other side, then a spin under his arm.

It shouldn't have been so easy. After all, the only person that she'd ever danced with was her own reflection, and yet... it was entirely natural to let Nathan lead her around the room.

His steps were sure, and she could feel the strength in his body. Clara wondered what he was like before his accident and just how strong he was. She'd seen how his clothes hung on his body; he'd very obviously lost weight. Granted, they didn't hang quite so badly since she'd started getting him food and cooked meals, but he still had a long path of recovery to go.

But none of his shakiness, none of his illness, nothing inter-rupted the smoothness of his steps as they moved. It was like...

Like they were floating.

It was like so many moments she'd dreamed of, even if there were no costumes, no lights or cameras. There was just her and her charming leading man, looking at her like—

Oh.

She'd automatically looked up at his face, not even thinking about it, and she'd expected to see a friendly but relatively neutral expression. Something that would ruin the fantasy she had going in her head.

But no, it wasn't that at all. He was staring down at her like she was the center of the world. Like someone was looking at her with a soft-focus camera and sparkles were gently drifting over her face.

That... that look wasn't fair. Not at all. It made her knees weak in a way that she hadn't expected, and suddenly she was very worried about her palms sweating too much.

Time stretched out, ebbing away like it didn't exist at all. It was just her and him, and nothing else. Moving across the floor, reality falling away, leaving just them, only them and—

Another thundering boom, four times louder than the last, ripped through the air, followed by the sound of shattering glass, the sheer shock of it tearing away whatever moment the two had been having.

"What was that!?"

22

Nathan

Nathan swept up the glass spread across his floor while Clara continued to tape a tarp over his busted window, the wind still wailing outside and the rain desperately trying to get in.

Dumb window. Dumb storm. Dumb *everything* that had ruined whatever had been happening between the two of them.

"You alright down there?" Clara asked from up on her ladder. As much as Nathan would have preferred for her to stay on the floor, it was much better for her to be up there than him.

"Yeah, I'm fine. It's just, you know, another thing on the list."

"Today really has been eventful, hasn't it?"

"That's one way to put it."

But he'd take all the mess again if it meant he could hold Clara like that a little longer.

Nathan was acutely aware of what he looked like. He was

scarred all over, with some of his features twisted and pulled by the grafts. He was more akin to a monster than a man, but when Clara looked up at him while he was dancing... well, it had been easy to forget about what he'd become. The world had fallen away just like she'd said, and although he was no leading man, he was so glad that, for a moment, she saw him as a worthy substitute.

But then the storm had gone and busted out part of his house. He really must have kicked too many puppies in a past life or angered some sort of storm spirit, because his luck couldn't be *that* bad.

"I'm almost done up here. Is the coast clear yet?"

"Almost," Nathan answered, redoubling his efforts on the glass. He knew he would be finding bits of it for ages and that he would probably need to wear thick shoes in his place instead of his house slippers or socks, but he wanted to get as much of it taken care of as possible, so Clara didn't step in any of it. Sure, he'd gone and fetched her the muddy boots she'd left by his door, but he didn't want anything getting up past the treads. "There. I think that's most of it for now."

"Fantastic. I'll vacuum in the morning. Assuming the power is back and all that."

"The morning, right. What time even is it?"

"I left my phone in the kitchen. You got yours?"

Of course, he had his. It was how he'd played the music to their little dance, after all. It had been a quick search to find the song, and he'd almost chickened out. But seeing Clara sitting there, dejection across all her features, wishing for something so simple as a dance... well, how could he refuse her?

And also, how blind were the neanderthals she went to school with? No one asked her to a dance? Utterly preposterous. Clara was sweet, kind, beautiful and clearly knew how to move on her feet. How could anyone look at her and find her lacking?

Totally blind, all of them.

So, despite his fear, despite his assurance that she would reject him, he'd asked her to dance with him. The beauty and the crippled beast. It was preposterous, really, but then her hand had been in his and it had been...

It had been...

It had been so *right.*

Maybe some would say that her touch was electric to him, but no, electricity wasn't his friend. Her touch had been like honey, warm and soothing, washing over his hurts with sweetness and healing until there were only good things left.

It was the first time that he'd been touched like that since his accident. Sure, he'd had his doctors and handshakes and physical therapy, but he hadn't been touched just for the sake of it, just to be close, since before his features had become marred. And then, the way she'd looked at him when she'd lifted her head. Now *that* was certainly something he'd never forget.

"Nathan?"

"What? Oh, right. My phone."

Setting his broom aside, he let out a low whistle. "I can't believe it. It's just past midnight."

"What, really? Man, I have completely ruined my sleep schedule. Usually, I'm up in the morning anywhere between four and six."

"Ah, I remember that life. Early to rise, early to get out of the heat."

"More like early to get out of my siblings' way. It's the best time for me to finish up my own chores so then they can do theirs."

"Well, it's safe to say that with this storm there probably isn't a whole lot of chorin' going on."

"No, probably not. I should text them again, let them know I'm still okay."

"Yeah, sounds smart." Nathan offered her his hand without thinking, but before he could doubt himself, Clara took it and climbed down the small ladder. "I'll go make sure the generator has enough fuel."

Clara nodded before letting out a truly loud yawn. It was so out of nowhere and her jaw opened so massively that Nathan couldn't help the chuckle he let out.

"You gonna make it to the kitchen there, Sleeping Beauty?"

And then he was blessed with that laugh again. Was he ever going to get tired of that? Unlikely.

"I think I'll be fine. Catch ya in ten."

"Yeah, catch ya in ten."

A large part of him didn't want to leave her alone, wanted to follow her to the kitchen and made sure she stayed safe. To let him bask in her presence a little longer. But he had a responsibility to take care of her, and part of that was managing the generator, so he was going to do just that.

Thankfully, it didn't exactly take long to do all that, and by the time he returned upstairs, he too was getting hit with exhaustion. He'd taken a nap, sure, but Clara hadn't been kidding when she'd called his day 'a lot.' Some sleep would do them both good.

"Hey. You still alive in there?"

Clara came out of his kitchen, drinking a cup of tea. He wasn't entirely sure of the scent, but if he had to hazard a guess, it was chamomile. "Oh, hey there. I'm just going to go crash on the couch."

"What? No. No way. You go take my bed."

She looked at him with wide eyes, like he'd just grown four extra arms and developed spider powers. "You need your rest, Nathan. You should sleep in your bed."

"I slept in it already today and there's no way, absolutely no way, I'm letting a guest of mine sleep on the couch."

"But—"

"Please, Clara. Let me be a good host."

At that Clara's mouth snapped shut and she nodded. "Okay. Thank you, Nathan. I'll take the bed."

"No problem. Besides, I've crashed on my couch plenty of times. It's par for the course for me."

"Okay. Do you want to get changed into your pajamas first?"

Nathan looked down, barely remembering he was just wearing his flannel pants and a loose T-shirt. Huh, he'd completely forgotten. "No, this should be fine. Already slept in it once, after all."

"Okay then. You don't mind if I..." She gestured to his shirt.

Nathan nodded—hopefully not too enthusiastically.

"Go ahead and sleep in that if you want."

"Okay, thanks, Nathan. I'll see you in the morning?"

"I wouldn't miss it."

She paused, looking up at him again. There wasn't much of a height difference between them, but it was just enough for her to tilt her head back ever so slightly. The tension between them was back, as it had been a couple times, but yet again something had shifted.

That seemed to happen between them often. Shifting plates, shifting tensions, nothing solid for him to stand on. It was uncertain, nerve-wracking, and always made him feel like he was about to make the wrong step. It should have been awful. Actually, it probably was.

The only hang-up about that, however, was that he was pretty sure he liked it.

Or at least he did until he remembered that a beautiful, rich woman like her wouldn't want anything to do with a scarred, crippled invalid like him.

Oh well, at least he could dream.

23

Clara

Clara tossed and turned for longer than she should have considering how exhausted she was. She had been so sure that she would just instantly fall asleep, but there was at least fifteen minutes of her staring at Nathan's ceiling just trying to get comfortable.

She couldn't believe that she was basically having a sleepover with an unmarried man. But she knew that nothing improper was happening between her and Nathan. Nathan knew it, and her family knew it. That was all that was important.

But still... something curling in her middle made her almost wonder if it would be so bad if... maybe... if something a little bit inappropriate happened, like a little kiss?

"Oh goodness. Get a hold of yourself, Clara."

Pressing her hands to her heated cheeks, Clara breathed in

through her nose and out through her mouth. It wasn't like she wanted to go in and jump his bones, or whatever it was the kids said, but she couldn't help but wonder what would have happened if their moment hadn't been interrupted.

Could they have kissed? Shared that intense moment before the entire screen faded to black? What would kissing Nate feel like? Would his lips be soft and warm? Would they be the same smoothness as the scars on his hand?

Thinking of that just made her cheeks burn redder and hotter, which made her writhe in the sheets. She could smell Nathan all around her, his detergent, his subtle cologne, that natural sort of masculine scent he had. It was... it was....

A temptation.

Clara had been tempted before. She'd gone on dates. After all, she wasn't a *total* spinster. But those dates had mostly been disappointing. She'd started later than all of her siblings, going on her first one when she was twenty-two and back from college, and when he'd gone to kiss her, she'd turned so he kissed her cheek. She just wasn't ready for that leap.

He hadn't called her back after that.

Clara wasn't beautiful like Charity or Cass. Sure, she had nice features, but she knew that wasn't what people saw first.

That was never what people saw first.

Maybe that was why she liked fashion so much and making her own clothes. Sure, she may not be the prettiest package, but she could wrap herself up in the finest bits and bobs, cover herself in ribbons until maybe, just maybe, someone would look at her like Marilyn Monroe or Elizabeth Taylor or Audrey Hepburn.

...Nathan kind of looked at her like that.

And that had her cheeks burning again. Oh, dear. She was going in circles. She needed a good night's rest and then maybe she could get her head on straight. Going back to some of her favorite songs, she hummed them gently to herself until she fell asleep.

When she finally did slip into slumber, her dreams were all about floating on clouds with a warm, strong hand in hers and a sturdy arm about her waist.

CLARA WOKE up to her alarm at first, but that lasted all of two minutes before she turned it off and fell right back under the covers. She didn't mean to, but the bed was so warm, and it smelled so nice. The next time she woke up, there was a gentle knock on the door, and she bolted upright.

"You back in the real world, Clara?"

"Huh? Oh, yes, I am! What time is it."

"It's nine AM."

Nine AM!? She couldn't remember the last time she slept so late! "Nine!? I need to call my family!"

"Is your phone charged?"

"Yes. My alarm went off before I—" Clara reached over to the nightstand and grabbed her phone, finding it was deader than dead. Drat. "Oh goodness. No, it's not. I need to charge it. I'm sure my siblings are worried sick!"

"Well, your brother hasn't come beating down my door, so I'm assuming they're not completely distraught. They might be dealing with storm stuff on their own."

"The storm! Right. Is it over?" Shaking her head, Clara tried to listen for the signs: the wind, the rain, the booming thunder. But all she heard was the gentle, ambient noise of a homestead.

"It's over. If you want, I just finished using my charger in the kitchen, if you wanna get your phone up 'n runnin' again." He moved to walk away, judging by the shadow of his feet under the door. Then he stopped and came back to the barrier. "I, uh, I made you breakfast."

"You what?"

"I made you breakfast. Nothing fancy, but I figured I'd at least return the favor."

There went her cheeks, burning again. He'd cooked for her? That was... that was almost like a morning after, except there'd been no 'night before.' It really was like something out of an old movie.

"I'll be right there."

"Okay." Another walk away, another return. What else could he want? "Oh, and you can use another shirt of mine, if you need, that is. I know it's not always pleasant having to stick around in dirty clothes."

"I can see your reasoning there. Oh! Is the power back? You know, since we're charging phones and all?"

She heard his gentle chuckle on the other side of the door. "Yeah, it's back. I took the liberty of putting your shirt and overalls in the wash with my outfit, but your, uh, your nicer clothes, well I figured it would be better off if I let you take care of those."

"I appreciate that! I do prefer to have the ones I make either dry cleaned or hung up on a line. The local dry cleaners absolutely loves me."

"Wait, you make your own clothes?"

It finally struck Clara as a little weird that they were talking through a door. "Yeah, just, you know, hold on one minute."

Slipping out of bed, she found where she'd discarded her leggings and hopped into them, practically tripping out of them. Normally they were things she liked to wear under her

dresses in colder weather, but she couldn't deny their useful-
ness and comfort when wanting to lounge.

But eventually she was able to get at least somewhat decent
—her hair was a right mess but there was no saving that—and
open the door.

"You really make your own clothes?"

"Well, not all of them, but a lot. It's surprisingly hard to find
clothes that fit me. Either they're too short, or they're too small,
or they're like a tent. And then you add that I have a somewhat... eclectic taste in fashion."

Nathan grinned at her happily, not like she was standing in
the door of his room with her morning hair, morning breath
and in his stolen clothes. "So, all of your outfits are one of a
kind?"

One of a kind? She'd never really thought of it like that.
"Uh, yes, I guess so."

"Makes sense."

And then he turned away and walked down the hall to his
stairs. Makes sense? Makes *sense?* What about it made sense?

She didn't ask that, however, and instead followed him
down the stairs and into the kitchen. Sure enough, there was
indeed food set out, some hash, some bacon and a nice
scramble with plenty of cheese on top. Now that was Clara's
type of meal.

"Oh yummy! Let's eat up!"

"The living room is a bit messy, so I guess we just eat right
here?"

"Sure, isn't the first counter meal of my day. I'm sure it won't
be the last. Although I will admit, I'm pretty spoiled by our
kitchen island to sit around. You remember it, right?"

"I remember it alright. Coulda fit a family of orphans
around it."

"But if they're orphans, they wouldn't have a family."

"What?"

Clara found herself smirking at him, just a bit. "You said a family of orphans. If they have a family, they're not orphans."

"Well, maybe they found their family in each other."

"Then they're not orphans, are they?"

"Aren't you awful witty for just waking up?" he said with a shake of his head. But it wasn't admonishing. It was more full of chagrin and amusement, which Clara found she quite liked.

"I like to think I'm always witty. I'm just less likely to hide it before I've had my morning tea."

"Well, lucky for you, I brewed more of that grey stuff you liked."

"You mean Earl Grey?"

"Yeah, isn't that what I said?"

Clara laughed, really laughed. It was loud and almost embarrassingly high pitched, but she couldn't help it. Maybe it was the adrenaline, maybe it was how awkward the situation was, but for some reason the innocent look he shot her with his flat tone just tickled her funny bone in all the right ways.

"You're absolutely right."

"You know, I don't get to hear that so often," he said, a soft smile across his features.

"I doubt that. You seem like a good egg, Nathan."

"A good egg? A scrambled one, maybe." He let out a huff of a laugh. "And speaking of eggs, we'd better start eating before breakfast gets cold."

"Sounds good to me."

They were relatively quiet while they ate, and once they finished, Clara wasn't quite certain what to do. But then Nathan took her empty plate and actually started to wash it in the sink.

His movements were sturdy and sure with no tremor to his hands.

Interesting.

"So," he said as he lathered them up. "You ready to go see what damage the storm did?"

Clara nodded. "Yes, I can do that."

As it turned out, the storm didn't completely ruin everything, but many of their seedlings were definitely washed out. They did their best to drain any water pooled in their containers, and Clara made sure to neatly gather them for planting in another day or so when the bed had time to dry.

The chickens, of course, were none too pleased. Especially since a branch had damaged the roof just enough to completely soak through one wall of nests. That took slightly more time, and it was halfway through cleaning *that* up when Clara remembered that she'd forgotten to text her family.

"Oh, my phone!"

She dashed to the kitchen and turned it on, the battery showing her that it was 100%. But then the boot up finished, and her notifications started pouring in.

Oh yeah, her siblings were definitely worried.

She called Papa first, and of course he picked up on the first ring. "Hey there, sunshine, are you alright? Charlie said you never messaged him about bringing your Jeep to Mr. Westbrook's place."

"I'm sorry, Papa. The storm blew out one of Mr. Westbrook's windows, so I stayed up late fixing it, then I slept through my alarm, and *then* my phone died while I was still snoozing."

"Wow. Sounds like quite the adventure. But are you alright? You know you haven't missed a night here at home since, well, since we took turns with your sister in the hospital."

"I know, Papa, but it wasn't safe to travel."

"It was pretty bad last night. But you are going to be heading home soon, right?"

"Once I finish up with the worst of stuff here, yes."

"Okay, sweetie. Love you, sunshine."

"Love you too." She was about to hang up when her father started to say something else. "I'm sorry, what was that?"

"I just... I just want to make sure that you're being careful."

"Careful?"

Her father sighed and it was such a melancholy sound. "You're a grown woman, Clara. If you're... if you're doing anything with Mr. Westbrook, I just want you to be careful."

"Doing... *Papa.* He was a perfect gentleman! He gave me his bedroom and stayed downstairs on the couch."

"Well, I'm right happy to hear that. But sunshine, I always want you to know that no matter what choices you make, you can talk to me. You'll never be alone."

Despite his strange and embarrassing assumptions, his words warmed her heart as her family's love always did. She was so lucky. "I know, Papa. And I promise, there is nothing going on between Mr. Westbrook and me."

"Alright then, I trust you, sunshine. I'll see you soon?"

"You'll see me soon."

Then he really hung up. Clara had to take a deep breath before she fired off texts to her siblings. Once that was handled, she tucked her phone away and went to help Nathan finish up.

24

Clara

*T*hings changed with Nathan.

It was subtle things, nothing too obvious, but every time she visited, she noticed something new. At first it was that sometimes, when she turned her head quickly, she would catch him staring at her. Perhaps it should have been creepy, but it wasn't. There was a gentleness to him that wasn't there before.

He started to get much less frustrated, even with himself, and he was much more complimentary. Sure, he still snapped at her occasionally, still called himself mean names from time to time, but those instances happened less and less. And when they did happen, he apologized for them almost immediately with no excuses.

And the nice thing was, with Mick recovered and the fall

season about to fully swing into gear, Clara was needed less and less back home, which meant she got to spend more time with Nathan without detriment to her family or her chore list.

They finished the garden, all of his seedlings fairly angry at how long it took them. There was definitely no way that Nathan would have been able to do it himself at all, so every time she looked at the increasingly green beds, she couldn't help but feel a warm, happy glow inside.

But once the garden was finished, it wasn't like there suddenly wasn't any work to do. In fact, they fell into a kind of a rhythm, a routine even. And while Clara never stayed the night again, she did stay plenty late when there was another thunderstorm. They were, after all, in the middle of the season for it.

She was well aware that some people would consider it improper.

The thing was, however, that she didn't hold much value to that opinion under the circumstances. Those people didn't see how scared Nathan still was during especially terrible storms. They didn't know how his breath would catch or how his face would go gray. And they didn't get to be there when there was a particularly bad boom of thunder and his hand would jerk out to grab hers without thinking.

But Clara was there for that, and Clara *did* hold his hand as long as he needed without comment. She wasn't going to give that up for anything.

Time passed, storms came and went. Before she knew it, the harvest was almost on top of them. So much had happened that sometimes she felt like she could barely keep up. Mick and Cass had gone on a couple of dates and that whole thing seemed to be going great. Clara wasn't sure if they were an item or not, but she was sure that Cass was incredibly happy. Like really happy. As in cheek glowing, heart racing, smiling all the time happy. Clara couldn't be more pleased for her sister. Cass deserved *so* much, especially after everything she'd been through, and it was nice to see her have some of her old joy.

...but Clara couldn't help but be a wee bit jealous.

She was elated for Cass; she was. She just, well, she thought it would be nice if she could have a little slice of the pie too. And sometimes, when she looked at Nathan, he looked like a particularly appetizing pie to dig into.

Of course, Clara tried not to think about that too often. Because if she did, she'd notice the strong profile of his jaw and the way the corners of his eyes crinkled when he smiled. And she was getting to see that smile far more often than before, the homesteader growing more and more open to her. He'd even stopped wearing those leather gloves of his around the house.

Although, sometimes when his mood was gloomier, she could feel him intensely watching her expression, like he was waiting for revulsion or rejection. During those moments, she did her best to keep her expression level and act completely normal. Besides, it wasn't exactly a trial. She was aware that he had scars, and she was aware that some people would be disturbed or disgusted by them, but to her... to her they were just stories.

Beautiful, intense, tragic stories written across his flesh in delicate filigree.

She remembered reading something about people who purposefully marred their flesh; it was called 'scarification,' and she couldn't help but think that even the best of them couldn't compare to Nathan's.

Maybe she was just biased.

Or maybe Nathan's own special Lichtenburg figures reminded her of the power of nature, the sheer might of the storm, but also his determination for survival. Maybe his skin grafts spoke of his dedication, his perseverance. Maybe he was mapped out with holy fractals drawn there by God to show the wonder of both his might and the might of his creations.

Clara much preferred the latter thought. She just wished Nathan could see himself the way she did.

"Hey there, you ready to harvest some beans?"

Clara looked up from the basket she'd been fetching from Nathan's tiny, run-down shed, barely managing not to shriek and jump in the air like a rabbit. "Yes, I am. Those beans are really having a good year, aren't they?"

"Ain't never seen nothing like it. What'd you put in that compost of yours?"

"Oh, just a lot of animal poop. A *lot* of animal poop."

"The best things in life can come out of a pile of sh—"

"*Nathan!*"

"Right. Pardon me, Clara. Bachelor life and all that."

"Mmmhmm," she said with a reproachful look as she handed him a basket. "Be careful or the next roast I make you might be full of soap."

"Hey now, it was an honest mistake. Ain't no reason to go messing with a man's meals. Besides, I'm pretty sure it'd be a sin to ruin something as delicious as one of your roasts."

"Who knows," she answered with a shrug, walking past him. Goodness, when she'd first started helping him there was no way they could have had such steady and even banter. Things really had changed between them. "Considering we make our own goats' milk soap, maybe you'd find that just as tasty."

"Goats' milk soap? Is that your secret then?"

Clara paused on her walk around the house. "Secret?"

"Yeah, for how you get your skin like that?"

"Like what?" she asked, tilting her head. Sometimes Nathan really did get on about the strangest things.

"I... uh, nothing. Nevermind. It was a bad pun that didn't work out."

"Aw, that's a shame. I love puns."

"Oh I know. That is a lesson I've definitely learned by now. A *painful* lesson."

Clara clicked her tongue because it was the only way she could hide how hard she was smiling. Maybe an outsider would think that their banter was more conflict instead of camaraderie, but it was what worked for them.

"Careful, or I just might leave you to harvest all these beans by yourself."

"And miss out on the results of all your hard work? I doubt it."

"You're lucky I do so love gardening."

"I reckon I'm lucky in a lot of ways."

Shaking her head, she started on one side of the trellises while Nathan started on the other. He had his cane with him, which made Clara feel better considering how much leaning was involved with the whole process. While Nathan moved around plenty, she'd noticed his balance went a little wibbly anytime his head went too far forward. She guessed it was something to do with his eardrums being damaged by the lightning strike, but she wasn't about to ask him the particulars of his health.

"Anyway, you said something about your brother and a rodeo?"

He remembered that? She'd only mentioned it in passing. "Yes! He helps them out once a month or so during the summer, but he mentioned that they've had two people move on and three injuries, so he might help them full time after the winter."

"That seems like a pretty serious thing."

"Does it? I've never really been one for rodeo."

"Not one for rodeo?" Nathan gave her an incredulous look. "Why not?"

"A lot of the animals are stressed. There's always the smell of stale beer. And there's usually at least one jerk who makes a scene. I go, you know, with Charlie to support him, but it's not pleasant."

She should have known better. "A jerk who makes a scene? What do you mean?'

"Oh, you know how people are." Clara wished that she had never mentioned it. Already her stomach was twisting, and she wanted to get back to the pleasant mood from just seconds earlier.

But Nathan's voice dropped low, as it only did when his temper was rising. "No. I don't. What do you mean?"

"Aw, come off it, Nate. You know."

"I don't."

Clara sighed. She could keep avoiding it, but she knew that would just irritate him. And she didn't know why she was being so cagey anyway. Nate saw her; he knew what she looked like.

"You know how it is. Someone behind you thinks you're too tall so they yell at you that you're in the way. Or they rest their feet on your back and get boot prints on your nice dress. Or someone bumps into you and calls you a cow, or someone drunk puts their hands where they shouldn't be, so either you or your sisters punch them out and then a whole brawl happens. You know, jerks causing scenes."

Nathan swallowed hard. "I... I don't like the sound of any of that."

Clara shrugged. "Just the realities of life. And it's not like something bad happens *every* time. It's just... enough times." She heaved another long sigh. "Besides, the animals really don't seem to enjoy it beyond the horses. Those are the only parts I like."

Nathan nodded gravely and she could see the storm rolling right across his expression. Funny, for a guy who definitely had PTSD involving lightning, he sure knew how to have a cloudy look. She needed to distract him, get his mind off things.

"Now, if you want to talk about rodeo *fashion,* that's something I can get behind. I love riding boots! They—"

Suddenly she was pelted in the face by something small and not that hard, cutting her off. Jolting, she looked down at the ground to see the mottled casing of a dragon tongue bush bean.

"Did... did you just bean me in the face?" she asked incredulously.

"Yeah," Nathan answered, the storm clouds gone and a cheeky grin on his face. "What are you gonna do about it?"

"What am I gonna do about it, huh?" She reached out and snatched a giant mountain pea pod, then chucked it at his face. He dodged, the son of a gun, but she was already reaching for the next one.

"Oh no, you don't," he growled, going for more as well.

And that was how the great bean war started. Clara dropped her basket, Nathan dropped his, and the greenery really flew. Clara laughed and laughed, even with beans hitting her in her face, getting into her hair and falling down her front. She practically was stumbling over herself, her muscles weak from her levity.

But it wasn't until she managed to get a beautiful trick shot into Nathan's open mouth when he taunted her, that she heard something truly wonderful.

Nathan *laughed*. Really, truly laughed. Not a chuckle, not a huff of a laugh, but a booming, reverberating bellow that sounded happier than she had ever heard him be. It made her heart leap into her throat and her blood sing in her veins. For a moment, there weren't any scars, there was no trauma, and they were just a couple of goofballs throwing food at each other.

And for a moment, everything was perfect.

25

Nathan

From the moment he saw Clara standing in the doorway of his bedroom, hair mussed from sleep and still wearing his clothes, he knew he was hooked. He'd never seen her so unkempt, but also never so beautiful. What little makeup had survived the rainstorm from the day before was smeared a little under her eyes, the fancy, styled curls atop her head had exploded into a wispy mess, and there was a slight smear of her obviously long-lasting lipstick where she'd drooled during the night.

She literally was the perfect woman.

And she could never be his.

That thought had stabbed right through him, into his heart, but he hadn't let it dampen his mood while she was there. If he was blessed with her company, then he was going to enjoy her company, and he would mope about it when he was alone.

The thing was, he was spending less and less time alone lately.

Instead of just coming over on Monday, Wednesday, and Friday for a meal, groceries and then some chores, she usually spent the entire evening with him, only heading home when it grew dark. And the weekends? She spent almost the entire Saturday with him and Sunday afternoon until around seven at night. She didn't ask him to go to church again, despite her deal, but Nathan wanted to work towards it.

Sure, he was still incredibly embarrassed that he'd had a panic attack at the church. It wasn't like he was scared of the church or anything. It was just that all those eyes on him, all that whispering, it made him feel like the worst sort of monster. The kind that the darkest parts of his mind liked to insist he was. It was like watching his self-perception crumple in on itself in real time.

And since he wanted so desperately for Clara to see him in a good light, for her to be proud of him, for her to see him as a decent and strong man, that rapid disintegration of how he pictured himself had been devastating. Crippling.

So, he drove to the church several times during the week and walked around the parking lot. He started on the edge, just strolling the perimeter. It was harder than he liked to admit, but if he went early or late enough, no one else would be there. After a week or so, he was able to move in closer. And then a touch closer.

Eventually, he could almost go up to the door. And then after that, he could touch the door. And while his little victories gave him hope, facing down an empty building was a whole lot easier than being inside of it when it was chock-full of congregants.

But he was going to keep trying. Because he'd given his

word to Clara, and after everything she'd done, she deserved at least that much. Nate may have been a broken man, but he wasn't a liar or a coward.

Or at least... not much of a coward.

So, time passed, he continued his work with Alejandro, and he increased his tele-health appointments with his therapist. The garden got planted, the roof of his chicken coop was fixed, and the fence posts of his pigpen were replaced one by one. His homestead had never looked so good or been so finely worked on.

But he never got to dance with Clara again.

He kept wanting to make it happen, kept dreaming of how perfect she'd felt in his arms, but the moment never really quite presented itself. And every time they did have a moment that seemed like it might be kind of right, he chickened out or something happened.

Okay, so maybe a little more of a coward than he would like to admit.

But he still cherished his time with Clara. He loved getting to know her. He found out more about her love of fashion, and she told him all sorts of stories about her own ranch.

He loved watching the glow in her eyes as she talked about her family, talked about their animals. He didn't understand how so much *goodness* could be in one package, but he guessed it made sense since it radiated out of her like the sun.

"What's the matter, out of ammo over there?"

Nathan ducked as another handful of beans was chucked at him. Sure, it was going to be tedious to pick all of them up later, but he didn't care. He was completely in the moment, wrapped up in Clara's laughter and that gorgeous smile of hers. It wasn't a dance, sure, but it was something between just the two of them.

Sure, the skin grafts in his shoulder were aching, pulling at his scar tissue, and yeah, he was a bit dizzy from the stimulation. But that was nothing compared to how his heart swelled from the sheer joy of it all, or how his stomach hurt from laughter. There was pain, but there was always pain in his life. What mattered was that the joy was finally louder.

"Oh, I'm just getting started!" he called back, grabbing some of his long pole beans and whipping them over the top of the plants at her.

It was silly. Ridiculous. And it was perfect. He was breathless, but he could hear her footsteps rushing around to the edge of the bed. Oh, she was going to rush him, was she? Well, two could play that game.

Nathan stood and lurched forward, his long legs taking him to the corner in two quick strides. It was possibly the fastest he'd moved since he was injured, and he miscalculated exactly how much ground his body would cover in those steps.

And of course, that miscalculation had him colliding directly with Clara as she went to rush around the corner and ambush him.

Hitting her was like hitting a wall, albeit a lovely, soft one, and his feet were knocked out from under him. He grabbed her on instinct and the two of them went tumbling to the side.

Thankfully it wasn't the worst fall, but they tumbled and ended up tangled in each other, his upper body across her middle and her elbow against his temple. It hurt, but it wasn't the worst.

Besides, it appeared that he'd fallen on quite the cushion.

"You okay?" he asked, righting himself. But his hand slipped on a bean and he caught himself on his own elbow, his face suddenly much closer to Clara's.

"Yes, I'm fine. It'll take more than a little tumble to hurt me. But what about you? You're not the first man I've bowled over."

"I have no problem believing that."

Clara chuckled easily. No recoil. No shudder at being so close to him. Just a cute little laugh. "I know, I know, with shoulders like these, who am I to waste them?"

"That's not what I meant," Nathan murmured. He felt his eyes scanning over every feature of her face, those petal lips of hers, those eyes, the way her round cheeks got even rounder with the way she was grinning.

"Then what did you mean?"

What did he mean? He meant that she was so beautiful he was sure there were plenty of men completely bowled over by the magnitude of her. By her beauty, by her intelligence, and by the kindness that surged out of her in innumerable ways.

But he didn't say that.

He wanted to say it. He wanted to tell her she was the best thing to happen to him in a decade and he would never be able to repay her for her kindness. That she made him want to be better. That he was so attracted to her that it physically hurt, and he would love nothing more than to dance with her, to kiss her, to hold her until she forgot about anyone who had ever hurt her feelings in her entire life.

But he didn't say that either.

"Nathan?" Clara asked, her brows furrowing a little like they did every time she was thinking.

He wanted to tell her that he wished he could be good enough for her. That he was a multimillionaire with a whole body instead of a cripple with PTSD and cobbled together from skin grafts both real and synthetic. He wanted to tell her that he wished he could have met her earlier, when he was himself and not the bitter thing he had become.

But he didn't say that either.

Instead, he said something completely insane.

"Would you like to go out with me?"

Oh *no.* That was not how that was supposed to go at all.

26

Clara

"Stop bouncing your leg, honey. It's going to be fine."

"Easy for you to say. You're not the one going on a date with the man you've had a crush on for months."

"Oh, for *months* now?" Charity asked with a raised eyebrow. "And here I thought I've been hearing you deny anything going on between you ever since that storm."

"That's because nothing *has* happened between us," Clara said, rubbing her stomach. She was nervous. *So* nervous. Her stomach was twisting, and her palms were sweating and—actually, she was pretty sure she was sweating *everywhere*. "Can you hand me the deodorant?"

"Girl, calm down," Cass said, using her walker to make her way to Clara's vanity. "You are the one who's way out of this guy's league. He's the one who needs to impress you."

"Out of his league?" Clara questioned, eyes wide. Had they

seen Nathan? He was tall with a cut jaw and a smile that could light up a room. He was rugged and tan, with thick hair and a love of animals that rivaled her own.

"Clara, honey, my favorite middle sister—"

"Your *only* middle sister," Clara interjected.

"Yeah, whatever. I don't know how you're unaware of it at this point, but you're a wealthy bombshell of a woman who could strut into almost any bar in the city and walk out with a beau on her arm."

Clara snorted, outright snorted. Sometimes her sisters said the craziest things. "Right. And I also can fly and breathe in space."

Charity clicked her tongue and sat on the edge of Clara's vanity. "Clara, come on. You have to understand how you look."

"Of course, I do. I am *acutely* aware of how I look. People like to remind me all the time."

"You see," Cass said, tone sharp. "I've seen men fall over you all of the time, and at least a dozen others have tried to ask you out at church or other functions. And yet your tone sounds entirely negative, so what's going on there?"

Clara heaved a sigh. She seemed to be doing that a whole lot more often than she would like to. She did *not* want to have this sort of conversation right before a date she was already nervous about. "Look, you guys are my siblings. You have to think I'm gorgeous."

"No, we have to love you. There's nothing in there about thinking that you're pretty," Charity said matter-of-factly. "Clara, do you not realize that you're a classic beauty?"

Clara rolled her eyes. "Just because I wear that fashion doesn't mean I—"

"For goodness sake, Clara. You have a face like an angel and a body—"

Charity held a hand up, cutting Cass off. "Clara, my dear, my sweet little sister. I know that people were cruel when we were younger, and I know that some part of our society says that you're not valuable because you're plus-sized, but surely you have to know now how utterly full of bull that all was."

Clara wrung her hands together, chewing at her lip. "Why are you guys bringing this all up now?"

Clara liked to think that she was a strong woman, a confident woman. She knew how to plant a garden, feed a family, and she knew how to make beautiful things. But suddenly, when faced with having a dinner with someone she was attracted to, all of her insecurities were surging to the forefront of her mind.

"Because we want to see you happy," Charity said, leaning forward to rest her forehead against Clara's. "And right now, you don't seem so happy."

"I'm just nervous. That's it."

"I really wish you could see yourself how we see you, Clara. You'd be amazed."

Clara let out a small chuckle and her eldest sister gave her a curious look. "It's nothing," she murmured. "I've just thought the same thing about Nathan many times."

"Is that so?"

"Yup."

"Well, I guess it would do you some good to listen to your own advice, would it not?"

She gave Charity a rueful look, but her sister just shrugged. "You may have a point, but I don't quite feel like admitting to that right now."

"Fair enough. How about we focus on doing your hair?"

Clara nodded. That sounded a lot better than whatever stressful conversation they were having.

And as she sat there, going through her makeup steps and her sisters somewhat helping, her mood did cheer up. It was almost ritualistic, the three of them going through a beauty routine together like they hadn't since their younger years. When she looked in the mirror, the three of them smiling and concentrating, she could see some of that beauty they talked about.

Classic beauty? Hardly. But she didn't need to put a bag over her head or anything. Yes... Nathan *was* lucky to go on a date with her.

But she still wasn't sure about that out-of-his-league thing. The only way she felt she outpaced him was in money and health, but she didn't like to use her family's wealth as a measure of her character. And considering that Nathan had been struck by literal lightning, she didn't think it was exactly fair to hold his health against him.

"I will never understand how you get your eyeliner wings so sharp," Cass said.

Clara grinned, her ruby red lips looking full and luscious in her mirror. Okay, it was definitely much easier to believe that she was gorgeous with a perfectly applied coat of long-lasting lipstick on. And although her sisters didn't share her love of makeup, it seemed that they were still happy to just enjoy the moment with her.

"It takes a lot of practice. I could teach you."

"No, thank you. I'll leave all of that to you. I have my own stuff going on."

"Dating an incredibly handsome cowboy isn't 'stuff going on,'" Charity teased with a laugh.

"Hey, I have other hobbies."

"Really? Name one."

Their banter faded into the background as Clara double-checked the waves and curls hugging her head. They were just big enough to be dramatic but not so overworked that they looked sticky with hairspray or like a wig.

"Alright, I'm going to get dressed."

Charity and Cass were still riffing off each other when she went to her closet. All of their brood were close, but Charity and Cassidy shared a special bond. If Clara had to guess, it probably was from both taking over to help the family after Mama had died. Papa tried his best, he did, but his heart had been so broken. There was only so much that he could do.

It'd been a long time since that whole tragedy had happened, and while Clara understood grief, she wished that maybe, just maybe, Papa could move on. It didn't seem healthy for him to be alone for the rest of his life, and she was sure that Mama would want him to be happy.

She was also sure that Mama would want *her* to be happy as well, but that was slightly more complicated. Clara always tried to do what brought her fulfillment, what brought her joy. She'd just long since settled with the fact that some of the things she wanted just weren't possible.

But Nathan made her wonder if some of them actually weren't as impossible as she had believed.

And perhaps that was why she picked out her favorite retro look. A royal blue dress with red piping along the Peter Pan collar and the pockets in her skirt. Clara made a point to sew pockets into almost all of her dresses, and it never failed to give her a smile every time she slipped her phone or wallet into them. Pockets were one of the best inventions in the world, and she resented just how much of women's fashion left them out.

Then her shiny red wedges with the black bows, and a ruby ribbon to tie into her hair. It all blended together into a seamless outfit that never failed to make her feel absolutely gorgeous.

And she needed all the confidence she could get.

"I think I see lights coming up the drive! Get ready!" Cass said, grinning devilishly from the window. The more serious she and Mick got, the less serious she grew in the rest of her life. And it was quite lovely.

Except when it was geared towards her. That part was less awesome.

"No way. Is it seven o'clock already?"

"Six fifty. Looks like Mr. Westbrook is a touch early, as every proper gentleman should be."

"Since when do you care about anyone being a proper gentleman?" Clara asked her eldest sister with a roll of her eyes.

"I don't. But you do, all that fancy old-timey etiquette and all that."

"Old-timey? Wow, you do know how to make a girl feel better, don't you?"

"What, it's the truth," Cass said with a grin. "You're a classic, and so you like classic things. Just because we don't have the same tastes doesn't mean we don't understand that it's important to you. And what's important to you is what's important to us."

That made Clara grin and some more of that nervousness faded. "Alright, how do I look?"

"Like a dreamboat."

"Yeah, what Charity said, a real dream. You sure that this Nathan guy is healthy enough for all that?" Cass made a gesture to Clara with wiggling fingers. "Because I think even a fully able-bodied man might have a heart attack when a literal movie star walks out the door to greet him for a date."

"Goodness, enough with the hyperbole. You're going to make me blush."

"Aren't you already blushing?"

"Artificially, yes. It's this new indie brand I found. Cruelty free and—"

Cass cleared her throat. "I think I hear the car pulling up now!"

"What? Really?" With one last pat of her hair, Clara rushed down the stairs. She wanted to get down to the ground floor before he came to the porch so she could catch her breath. The last thing she wanted to do was be panting when she opened the door.

"Whoa there, sunshine. You look lovely."

Clara blinked at Papa, trying to catch her breath from running down the stairs in her wedges. She knew better than that; that was how twisted and broken ankles happened.

"Oh, hey, Papa. Thank you!"

"That's your favorite dress, isn't it?"

Clara nodded, still trying to steady her heart.

"This Mr. Westbrook fellow must have really turned himself around."

"He has, Papa."

"That's good to hear. I'd hate it if you were caught up in trying to save him to the point of ignoring red flags."

Now that was enough to narrow her eyes at him. "That's not the case, Papa."

"That's good. I'm glad to hear that."

"You may be glad to hear that, but do you actually believe that? Do you believe me?"

His expression softened. "I do believe you, honey. I just want to make sure that you've thought things through from every angle."

"I understand, Papa, and I appreciate that. But it's not like we're running off to elope. It's just a date."

"Just a date," he repeated, giving her that sort of fatherly knowing look that only dads had. "I knew I was going to marry your mother from our very first lunch together."

"Well, you and Mama were meant to be. The two of you were..."

"Classic?"

Clara couldn't help but grin at that, even with tears pricking at the corners of her eyes. "Yes. Classic."

A knock sounded on the door, interrupting anything else that might have made the moment even more beautifully bitter-sweet, and Clara jolted.

"It's him!"

"Alright, let me open the door, sunshine. You stand right there so I can see his face when he gets a look at you."

"*Papa,* you're going to embarrass me."

"Honey, I would be surprised if Mr. Westbrook even realizes that I'm here."

Clara felt her cheeks burn again. Her family was so over-the-top about such things. It was nice, but it still embarrassed her from time to time.

But she didn't have much time to think about it because Papa was opening the door, and there Nathan was.

Goodness.

Since she'd met him, Nathan had worn either oversized flannels and his thick jeans, usually with his leather gloves and the cap he often used to hide his face. Once, on that fateful sleepover, she'd seen him in just a T-shirt and flannel pants, but that was it.

But Nathan wasn't wearing anything like that now. Instead, he was in dark dress slacks with a slate-gray formal shirt, a single onyx tie. No hat, no gloves, dark cowboy boots that didn't have a lick of dirt on them. His hair had been cut and brushed back, far from the overgrown mop she'd grown used to seeing, and, she couldn't say how, but there was a brightness to him.

And a whole lot of nerves.

Maybe it was mean, but it made her feel better that he was clearly as nervous as her. It was written into the wrinkle of his brow, the slight flutter to his hands and the way that his tongue would quickly come out to swipe along his lips. Clara was reminded of just how much she thought he had *very* nice lips.

"Hello there, Nathan," she murmured, standing a few feet past her doorway, Nate frozen on her porch.

He didn't answer at first, his Adam's apple bobbing up and down several times. It almost grew to the point of being awkward, but Papa cleared his throat and that seemed to jolt Nathan back to life.

"Hello, sir," Nathan said, holding out his hand to shake Papa's. "I'm Nathan Westbrook. Pleased to meet you."

Papa reached out and shook his hand. "Good evening, Nathan. I've heard a lot about you."

Nathan's eyes flashed with concern. Then he once again turned his attention to Clara.

"Clara. Y-y-you look amazing."

Her first instinct was to tell herself that he was wrong, that he was just buttering her up. But so much of what her siblings said stuck with her, along with Papa's kind words, and she decided that maybe, maybe it wouldn't be so bad to pretend that she thought of herself the same way they did.

"I do, don't I?" she said, giving a twirl.

Nathan let out a nervous laugh and finally stepped over the threshold of the house. "You really do. Did you make that?"

"I did. How can you tell?"

"Mostly a guess, since it fits you like a glove and all."

"Good to hear you complimenting my daughter's excellent craftmanship," Papa said with another dad look, although entirely different from his previous dad look. A sort of dad look that made her think of shovels and implicit warnings. "Because I'm sure that's what you were complimenting, right?"

"Yes, of course." Nathan sputtered, and Clara thought how cute it was how his cheeks went a little red. At least she wasn't the only one blushing. "I couldn't do anything like that. I'm lucky I can reattach my buttons and patch stuff on my jeans."

Papa nodded in approval. "It's good that you can do that. I know far too many people who are helpless when it comes to repairing their own clothes. It's a valuable skill. They should have never taken it out of school."

Nathan nodded, and Clara could tell from his expression that he didn't know quite what to say about that. Maybe she should rescue him, but it was still quite entertaining to see him squirm a little.

And also, maybe some small part of her brain was pleased to see that he was willing to go through so much for her. She was well aware that Nathan wasn't exactly the most social sort, and the fact that he was standing in the middle of her house, undisguised and trying to be on his best behavior, well it meant a lot to her. A whole lot.

But, considering just how much they'd been through together, she also knew that she didn't want to stress him out or agitate him. Nathan's self-image was even shakier than hers, and she didn't want to punish him for being brave enough to show up without his usual wrappings.

"Why don't we get going, Nathan?"

He shot her such a relieved look that Clara felt maybe a wee bit guilty that she'd been enjoying his bewilderment. "Yes, that would be great. I assumed I'm driving?"

"I would love that, thank you."

He offered her his arm, and for once, there was no flinching when she tried to touch him, no hesitant wait for a rejection. Instead, he just grinned at her, and the two of them left together.

When they reached his car, an older sort of junker that looked like a whole lot of love had been poured into it, he let go of her to open the door for her. That probably shouldn't have made her heart patter, but it did, and she flushed as she lowered herself into the vehicle. Not exactly the easiest thing to do in wedges and her rockabilly dress with a medium petticoat underneath, but she managed to do it without looking like a completely uncoordinated lamb just learning to walk.

It didn't take long for him to circle around, and Clara noticed that he wasn't using his cane. She hoped he didn't feel like she thought less of him when he used his mobility aides. Her own sister still wobbled between her chair, walker and cane all the time, and Clara was grateful they lived in an age where such medical devices were available.

But then he was inside, and they were driving off, an indistinct sound playing over the radio.

Clara didn't know what to say, and clearly Nathan didn't either, because they were both quiet on the drive into town. It wasn't a long one, just ten minutes of comfortable quiet, but it was nice. It reminded her of when they would garden or do chores together. Just working hard while enjoying each other's presence.

When they did pull up into the parking lot of one of the two restaurants in town, the mood shifted noticeably for her. She could feel it prickle across her skin like an electric current.

"Are you alright, Nathan?"

He was staring at the restaurant, slightly leaning forward over his steering wheel. She could feel the tension radiating from him, which made her wonder if accepting his offer for a date had actually been selfish.

No. She couldn't think that. Nathan was a grown man and didn't need to be infantilized like that. He believed that he was ready to go on a date with her. He'd been incredibly genuine when he asked, after all. And while she didn't quite understand it, she respected him enough to believe him.

"I... this is the first time I've gone out in public like this."

"Since the accident?"

"Yes. Since the accident."

Clara swallowed, her heart aching for him once more. With all those layers peeled back, he was exactly the kind, funny person she'd always known was under all the spite and misery, and he didn't deserve the lot he was handed.

"We don't have to go in, you know," she murmured, laying a hand on his knee. The touch was like fire up her palm and it made her blood sing. That was... that was something. She'd felt something like that before when they'd touched, but it was entirely more potent.

Nathan took in a few deep breaths and she watched how his chest rose and fell. "No. I want to do this. I want to show you—" He cut himself off, shaking his head.

"You wanted to show me what?" Her tone was low, unassuming, she hoped. She felt like something tremulous was unfolding between them, something delicate that needed to be protected.

Once more, Nathan didn't answer right away. He licked his lips, drummed his fingers against the steering wheel, and fidgeted in his seat. Clara let him get all of that out of his system. She figured that either he would tell her or say no, but she needed to give him the time to come to his own conclusion.

"I want you to see that I can be a leading man. Or at least something like that."

Oh.

Oh.

Forget about cheeks flushing. Her whole body simmered with a warm blush. He... he wanted to be that for her? He didn't think that her fantasies of older times, that her love of all things retro and classic was silly or antiquated?

"I think that's the nicest thing anyone outside of my family has ever said about me."

"Really? Well, that's a right shame." He took another deep breath and it seemed that her words bolstered him. "That does it. Let's have dinner, shall we?"

"Are you sure?"

He turned to her for the first time since they pulled in and the expression on his face took her breath away. There was just so much there: fear, admiration, anger, caring, regret, adoration. It was a heady mix, and for a moment she felt frozen in some metaphorical headlights.

"I am. I want to do this. I want to take you on a date because that's the bare minimum of what you deserve."

"Oh geez, I don't know about *deserving.*"

But his tone was completely serious when he spoke next. "I do."

Oh goodness, what was she supposed to say to that?

"Okay. Let's have dinner then."

He nodded, then got out of the car. Clara went to follow, but then Nathan was suddenly at her door, opening it for her and offering his arm. She took it, tucking her head slightly to hide her giddy smile. Maybe some people needed more glitz and glam, but to her, the night was unfolding like the perfect dream.

Just her, dressed in her best, and Nathan, dressed in his best, with eyes only for each other. She could almost hear the music playing in the background.

...that might actually be a bit unhealthy. Oh well. She was from a family of millionaires; she could afford to be a little eccentric.

And so, they entered the restaurant with a smile on her face. The hostess hardly gave them a second look, keeping her customer service smile in place without so much as a wobble. Good for her. Clara would make sure to leave her an extra tip before the end of the night.

"A booth in the back, please," Nathan said. And although she could hear the nerves in his voice, the young hostess didn't seem to catch it at all and led them to their seat without missing a beat.

Yes, a *very* extra tip.

She could tell Nathan was apprehensive as they sat there, using his menu as a sort of shield and ducking down. It made her heart throb yet again, that there was so much struggle to him just living his life, but she was so incredibly proud of him for the fact that he was trying.

"We can bail at any time," she assured him.

"No, I want to do this. Appetizer?"

She nodded, picking up her own menu, even though that was just for show. With only two restaurants in their town, she had pretty much memorized their entire menu over the years.

The waitress joined them soon after and she, too, didn't stare, jolt or otherwise act like Nathan was anything other than a handsome patron at her place of work.

It was all going great. Wonderfully even. Until suddenly a hand was on Nathan's shoulder and both of them jolted.

"Oh, Mrs. Hernandez!" Clara exclaimed, recognizing one of the older church patrons. "How nice to see you!"

"Yes, nice to see you, Miss Clara. And you, Mr. Westbrook. We've been praying for you, you know."

Nathan was looking down at the table, his lips pulled into a tight line. "Thank you. I appreciate your kindness."

"Of course, dear. With God's grace, we all have faith you'll be restored."

He almost managed to completely hide his grimace, and Clara quickly tried to swoop in to the rescue.

"Thank you so much, Mrs. Hernandez. But if you don't mind, we just wanted to enjoy a quiet meal to ourselves."

"Right, right! Naturally. It's so sweet of you to make sure our Mr. Westbrook here had someone to dine with."

"What? No. This isn't anything like—"

But she was already bustling off and Clara felt a wave of uncharacteristic anger churning through her stomach. "Why are some people so *ru*—"

Nathan just waved his hand. "It's fine. I can't blame her for thinking that. It's a severe understatement to say that you're out of my league."

"What? No, I'm not!" *Why is that the second time I've heard that today?*

But Nathan just grinned at her, like he knew something she didn't. "Okay."

She didn't have time to argue because then their food was arriving. Just an appetizer, but it was still enough to make Clara lose track of exactly what point she was trying to make.

Except then another hand came up and clapped Nathan on his back.

"Hey there, buddy! I ain't seen you in a right minute!"

Of course, it was another church-goer. And of course, he was happy to loudly proclaim that he was praying for Nathan's recovery. Maybe they could have just moved past that, but barely more than a minute after he left, Mr. and Mrs. Haversbrugen came up to give him their well wishes.

"What, is everyone in town here tonight?" Clara found herself muttering. She meant it to be amusing, but Nathan was sitting stock still, his only movement being his jaw flexing as he ground his teeth together.

Drat. Not even really good food was going to fix that kind of tension. Anxiety rolled up her throat and she felt her stomach roil.

"Hey, I know that you wanted to do this to prove something to me," she whispered. "But you don't have anything to prove at all. I admire you so much, Nathan. And if you want to get out of here, then we can just go. I don't mind at all."

His eyes flicked up to her and she felt the guilt in them. She just wished that Nathan could give himself a break. He tried *so* hard.

"You don't?"

"No. To be honest, not getting to have a conversation without well-meaning busybodies interrupting is kinda ruining the experience."

He heaved a huge sigh of gratitude and pulled two twenties to set on the table. "I'm sorry, Clara."

"You don't have anything to apologize for, Nathan. But would you mind pulling the car up? I underestimated how much my feet were going to ache."

"Sure, alright. I can do that for you, no problem."

He looked more than happy to hurry off. Clara waited until he was out of sight to put a hundred-dollar bill just under her plate and then hurry to the front. Thankfully, the same hostess was there, and Clara hastily handed her one as well.

"What the—are you serious!?" she cried, looking at Clara with wide eyes. "You can't be serious."

"I am. I just wanted to thank you for your graciousness and professionalism. I won't forget this."

"I... I don't know what to say!"

"Don't say anything," Clara assured. "Just pass the kindness along some day if you can. And—oh, look. There's my ride! You have a good night now."

Clara hurried out before a real scene could happen, and sure enough Nathan was right there, already holding her door open. Clara slid right in without a hitch, and once Nathan was in, they were off.

Once more, they didn't say anything, but the pleasant and comfortable mood was gone. No, there was a tension there and all of it was radiating from Nathan. Clara wished she could fix it, but she didn't know how.

"I'm sorry, Clara. I really am."

He sounded so dejected, so miserable. Clara hated it. "You know what? Turn right."

"What?"

"Turn right. There's somewhere I want to show you."

"You don't want me to take you home?"

Clara shook her head. "You promised me a date, right? Well, that was hardly a date."

There it was, the tiniest of grins making its way across his features. "Alright then."

"Don't worry. It won't take long."

"I'm not worried. I trust you."

Clara didn't even try to fight the smile that spread across her face, settling in for the short ride to the destination she had in mind. It was just starting to get dark, but not so much that they couldn't see. It was that coppery-warm sliver just between day and twilight, when everything got a little soft and it seemed that magic just might be possible.

"Here, pull off here."

"Here? There's no road."

"I thought you said you trusted me," she shot back coolly.

He narrowed his eyes at her, a quip clearly on his tongue, but instead he just turned where she'd pointed. It was bumpy, that was sure, but less than a moment later, they were right where she wanted.

"Stop here."

"Here? There's nothing here."

"Oh, ye of little faith," Clara chided, opening her door for the first time that night. Once she was out, she kicked off her shoes, knowing just how dangerous it was to walk across uneven ground in heels.

Nathan followed her, although there was curiosity written all across his face. It was much better than the abject misery that had been there before, of course.

"So why have you led me to an empty field? Do I need to be worried about any old-fashioned mob movies you've been watching?"

"Hah! No, nothing like that. I was just thinking..." Turning to him, she offered her outstretched hand. "It would be awfully nice to dance again."

27

Nathan

𝓝athan had been so sure that his one chance at a date with Clara was an utter failure. He'd beefed it, he really had. Why would beautiful, confident Clara want to date a man who was defeated by a simple restaurant?

He'd tried. He had tried *so* hard, but every time a someone came up and wished him God's blessing, he crumpled a little inside. And that old rage that was so familiar to him grew a little bigger in his chest.

God's blessing, huh? If God wanted to bless him, then why did the big guy let him get struck with lightning? What could he have possibly done to deserve having so much lightning go through him that his skin caught fire from the inside out? So that his organs nearly went offline permanently, and his nervous system got so scrambled that it took months of physical therapy to walk again.

God's blessing? More like God's curse.

Nathan wished he could just brush away that anger. That bitterness. Tell those dark thoughts inside of him where they could stick it. But he couldn't. It was like they'd rooted into his soul and wouldn't leave.

But then, right when he was admitting defeat and driving home, Clara had asked him to take a different path. Of course, he took it. It was the least he could do. But then they were in a field and she was holding her hand out to him, looking like the most beautiful dream he'd ever had.

It wasn't fair, really, how incredible she looked. Her royal blue dress fitting her figure just right, her hair done how she liked, and those incredible ruby lips pulled into a warm grin just for him. She was a movie star, too perfect to be real, and yet she was asking to dance with him.

Him.

He would be insane to say no, so he didn't.

"I think so too," he said, voice low. Barely a whisper. But she clearly heard him because her hand was in his and she was closing the distance between them. "What about music?"

"I have that handled," Clara said, slipping her hand into the pockets sewn to the front of her dress and pulling out her phone. He watched as she typed in a few words, and then a bluesy, romantic melody drifted out of the speaker. "I think that'll do," she murmured before sliding the phone back into her pocket. "Shall we dance?"

Suddenly, he very much couldn't speak, so he didn't even try. He slid one of his arms around Clara's waist and started leading her in the only steps he knew.

They moved together so easily, like they'd been dancing together for years. Which was ridiculous since Nathan only knew most of the moves from his grandmother. Every New

Year's they would dance the last few minutes of midnight away, for good luck, and then on her birthday too. She'd always said that she was giving him an advantage for any woman he met in the future, and she apparently was even more right than she knew.

But even with every advantage he had multiplied by two, he still didn't measure up to the force of goodness that was Clara Miller.

He wished he did; he really did. But if wishes were fishes, then he'd find his fortunes in the sea.

"Thank you," Clara said as they strode across the field. The sun had sunk further in the few moments that they'd stepped out of the car, backlighting the woman like she was some sort of celestial being.

"For what?"

"For being brave enough to ask me out."

Brave? Is that what she thought of him? Brave was just about the last thing he felt he was. But if Clara believed that, maybe he could be a little braver for a few more moments.

"Clara..."

"Yes, Nathan?"

He swallowed again. Was the air suddenly dry? It felt dry. Or maybe that was just his tongue.

Or maybe it was just everything that was Clara. Her beauty, her kindness, all of it was so overwhelming and yet he never wanted it to go away. He wanted to bask in it forever even though he didn't deserve it. Even though he was full of tension, bitterness and anger.

Because, with Clara, it felt like maybe he could be better. That one day all that darkness that clung to him *would* be gone.

"Nathan?"

Right, he needed to say something. He needed to be *brave.*

"Look, I know that I'm not good enough for you. I'm not clue-less. But I hope you know that I really, really, *really* wish I was."

"Oh, Nathan..."

He knew that tone. It was pity. He should have known better than to say anything, but she'd thought he was brave and so he'd wanted to be just that. But then she kept on talking.

"You're a good person. You really are. And I just wish you could see that."

He didn't know what to say to that, his breath hitching. "I'm not—"

"But you are. And yes, you have flaws, and yes, you have bad habits. You have wounds that seep outwards and hurt people around you. But you're healing. And you're working on yourself. Every day.

"Don't think I don't see it. Because I do. I notice all the ways you've already improved, and I believe you can do so much more."

She believed in him? Sure, she was letting him down, but it was a gentle, kind rejection. Of course, Clara would be cour-teous and thoughtful even in telling him he had no chance. He should have known.

But he wasn't bitter about it, strangely enough. Sure, it made his heart ache, but it also filled him with hope. Because there was no revulsion in her voice. No disgust. Just kindness.

"Thank you, Clara—"

"Hey, I wasn't done talking." Her reproach was still just as sweet, but firm.

"Sorry, continue," he said, then snapped his trap shut.

"I was saying, I believe you can do so much more, and I believe that you can keep healing. And, as long as you're willing to keep working on being the best you that you can be, I'd like to be right there with you."

He faltered in his steps, nearly tripping over his own feet in shock. He knew he was staring openly, but he felt like his brain was suddenly on the fritz. Surely... that couldn't mean what he thought it meant.

"Y-you what?"

"I would like to go on this journey with you, Nathan. I don't want you to be alone."

But she couldn't mean that! She couldn't! He had nothing to offer her at all.

She continued, "And before you accuse me of doing it for charity, it's not that. I get something out of this too. I get a *lot* out of this."

What could she possibly get out of it? Nathan must have fallen and hit his head. Oh well, if he was stuck in a hallucination, it was a pretty nice one to have.

"I like spending time with you, Nathan. And when I help you on your homestead, I feel like I'm actually doing real, hard work. I feel appreciated. Valued."

Of course, she was appreciated and valued. He'd probably be dead three times over if it weren't for her. She'd saved him, literally.

"Remember when I told you my fantasy about walking into a big dance hall and having that magical moment? You were the first person who *got* it. And in that moment, I felt so *seen.* You understand me in a way that nobody outside of my family does.

"And even though my family loves me, and they respect my passions, they don't *get* it. But you, *you*, Mr. Nathan Westbrook, you said you wanted to be my leading man. You *understand* me."

Somehow, during her words, she'd closed the slight distance between them even further. Without her heels, she was just short enough that she had to tilt her head upwards to look at him.

Cheeks pink, lips ruby red, eyes smiling. He had never wanted to kiss someone so much in his life, and he'd kissed quite a few pretty ladies in his early twenties, before he realized he preferred the quiet life over flying fast and loose.

"You think I could be your leading man?" he whispered, his voice sounding ragged to even himself.

"If you think I could be your leading lady."

"Clara, I've never met more of a star. You're incredible. Incredible doesn't even do it justice."

The first fledgling starts of the twilight that had just barely begun to emerge stood reflected in Clara's eyes as she gazed up at him. He saw so much in their depths, affection, attraction, admiration, but none of the ugly, vile things his mind told him he should find there.

Could it really be that a rich, beautiful woman with nothing but kindness written into her bones could ever want something like him? That he could be more than a charity project that she took pity on?

It seemed so. As impossible as it was to believe, he owed believing Clara if she said she wanted to be with him.

"That's the second nicest thing anyone's ever said to me."

"Oh yeah? And what was the first?"

"What you said in the car just a little bit ago."

So much rushed through Nathan as he held Clara, the two of them having completely forgotten the music and just gently rocking side to side. His heart felt like it was swelling in all the right ways and he never wanted to stop. He could burst to ash in her radiance, and that would be just fine with him as long as he got to stay by *her* side.

"Clara?"

"Yes?"

"I'd really like to kiss you right now." His voice was less than a whisper, barely more than a rumble, but somehow, she seemed to hear it because a soft, sweet smile spread across her face.

"You know, I've never been kissed. Not a *real* kiss."

"Well, everyone should get to have at least one *real* kiss."

"Is that so?"

"Yeah, that's so."

"Well then," her voice was just as breathless as his, and the increasing starlight drenched her features in the gentlest of silvers. "What are you waiting for?"

"What indeed?"

Dipping down, he pressed his mouth to hers. Her lips were soft, so incredibly soft, and warm against his own. A slight sigh escaped her mouth and then she practically melted into him.

Suddenly, his body was alight in all of the best ways possible. Every bit of his skin felt like it was electrified, and for once that wasn't his worst nightmare. It was almost like he was a normal man, a real man, blood racing in his veins and heart calling out for everything that Clara was.

He clung to her, and her to him. He wanted to get lost in her until there wasn't a single bit of darkness inside of him. He wanted to fight and heal and be exactly what she deserved.

They parted for just a moment, and when he looked down at her face, he saw just how breathless and beautiful she was. It was certainly... affecting.

"How was that?" he asked.

"I'm not sure," she whispered, and for a moment his blood ran cold. But then she kept on speaking and he realized that he should have known better. "Maybe we should try it again to make sure we got it right."

He grinned. He still couldn't believe it, still half expected to wake up in his bed covered in sweat and all alone.

But he wasn't alone. He had Clara in his arms, and she didn't want him to go away. In fact, she wanted to kiss him again.

So why wasn't he kissing her already?

A terrible oversight on his part. One that he solved by pressing his lips to hers once again.

He didn't know what he'd done to deserve her, but he was going to spend the rest of his life making sure that he was good enough to keep her.

28

Clara

"Youre *what* now?"

Clara looked calmly at her younger brother, who was about one step away from choking on his minty milkshake.

"I'm dating Nathan Westbrook, and I wanted all of you to know."

"About time," Cass said with a grin. "You've been lovesick for weeks now."

"Well, I don't know about *lovesick*," Clara answered. "But yes, our date went well, and I've decided that we're in a good spot to pursue a relationship."

"In a good spot to pursue a relationship," Chastity teased. "Have you ever heard a more romantic overture?"

"I'm trying to be practical about this."

"Ah yes, practicality, the cornerstone of romance."

Clara shot her sister an exasperated look. She knew the eldest was teasing her, judging by the twinkle in her eye and the quirk to the corner of her lips, but Clara was very much trying to be serious.

Maybe it was a strange tactic to tell her family while at dinner, but she wanted to be up front with them. She'd been denying that there was anything between her and Nathan, and while that had been accurate at the time, it wasn't anymore.

Sure, she'd kept it quiet for about two weeks after their first date, just to make sure that Nathan wouldn't suddenly get cold feet or anything of that nature. But after two more dates, each more wonderful than the last, she was absolutely sure that they were going to be a thing for a while. And she wasn't going to lie to her family, even through a lie of omission.

After all, she might have been many things, but she wasn't a liar.

"Hold on, how are all of you taking this so lightly? Clara is dating Mr. Cranky McCranky pants after spending most of the fall telling us how awful he is, so what's the deal?" Charlie's brow was furrowed, and he was fidgeting in his chair, like he wanted to stand up but knew that would be a touch too dramatic.

He wasn't quite angry, Clara could tell, but he certainly wasn't happy. Not that she could entirely blame him. He had a point about Nathan being pretty rude, and it was only natural that he would be concerned for her.

That was probably mostly her fault. Since Nathan had started changing, she'd talked about him less and less. She hadn't thought about it at the time, so wrapped up with the conflicting feelings in her own chest, but in retrospect, she should have been just as vocal about the good things as she had about the bad things.

"The deal is he's changed, and he's been changing. I just... perhaps was not as forthcoming about that part."

"Clara, I love you, I really do, but you tend to see the best in everyone. You said this guy just watched as you had to fight off a coyote in a pigpen. How am I supposed to trust him to protect you? To have your best interest at heart?"

Ouch. She knew that story was going to come back to bite her. "I know that things started off rocky, but believe me when I say he's made such an amazing effort. He was in a bad place, a real bad place, and he just needed someone to be there for him."

"And of course, that someone has to be you." Charlie let out an aggravated sound. "Clara, you've got a heart a mile wide and I love that about you, but I'm worried. Like really worried. You don't have to save everyone—"

"*Charlie.*"

The whole conversation froze at Papa's low words. He'd been sitting silently at the head of the table, and Clara had almost been afraid of what he might say.

"What?" her brother finally said cautiously.

But Papa didn't answer for several long beats, looking over each one of them before his gaze landed on Clara.

"Clara, do you believe that Mr. Westbrook is a good man?"

"I do."

"And do you understand why we would be worried?"

"I do."

"And you have feelings for this man?"

"I do."

"And he treats you right?"

"He does."

Papa gave one long, slow nod. "Then what else do we need to know? I trust Clara's judgment."

"B-but," Charlie objected, sounding miserable. "What if something happens? I don't trust this guy! I feel bad for him, being struck by lightning and all, but that's not carte blanche to be a...a... well, to be such a jerk!"

"*Charlie,*" Clara said firmly.

"I know you don't like hearing that, sis, but seriously. What if he hurts you?"

"Then we'll be here to support her," Papa said, just as firm as before. "Because that's what family does."

Charlie settled back in his chair, but he still looked quite stressed. Maybe if he was angry or belligerent, she'd be annoyed with him, but clearly it wasn't rage fueling him. Poor Charlie almost seemed scared, and Clara wished she understood where that fear was coming from.

"The question is, my boy, do you trust your sister?"

"I... I do."

"Then trust her."

Charlie didn't reply right away to that, chewing his lip. The table was tense, that was for sure, and Clara was grateful that Cass and Charity were just observing rather than pitching in. The two could be overwhelming as a combined force, and she wanted to understand her brother, not bludgeon him into submission.

"I... okay. I trust you, Clara. But if anything goes wrong, you gotta tell us, okay?"

"Of course," Clara said, standing. "I will always be as honest with you as I possibly can."

Charlie's expression was still one of absolute misery, so Clara crossed around the table to kiss his forehead. "I'm being safe, little brother. I promise. He would never intentionally try to hurt me."

"People can trick you, you know. You think you're safe and then..."

Gently, she ran her fingers through the top of his hair. Given that he was the tallest in the family, it was easy to forget that he was the second youngest, but in moments like these it was easy to see the youth in him.

Out of all of them, Charlie was the most attached to family, the most dependent on ranch life. He had maybe one friend outside of the house and didn't really do anything other than the rodeo. He wasn't into church, the bars, or most other things young men his age loved. If she recalled right, he'd gone to the city maybe twice in as many years to hang out with other folks he knew.

And Nathan, for all his growth, was about as far outside of their ranch as someone could be. It made sense he'd seem upsetting to Charlie. Alejandro and Savannah came over to the ranch more often than not, and Mick literally lived there. Meanwhile, Nathan usually drew Clara away for hours and hours.

"I know, Charlie. But that's not the case here. You just have to trust me. Can you do that?"

More chewing on his lip before finally he let out a long sigh. "Yeah. I'm sorry, Clara. I'm just..." He trailed off, and Clara gave him a one-armed hug.

"It's okay. Growing pains, right?"

"Yeah, growing pains."

Finally, the matter seemed to be settled and Clara returned to her seat. Perhaps it was a bit dramatic of her, but she waited until they all had picked up their utensils and started to eat before speaking again.

"I'm glad we're all agreed, because I'm inviting him to dinner here next Friday."

"You're *what?*"

"Hey, Nathan, I have something to ask you."

Clara swung her feet as she sat atop his kitchen counter, kicking her feet as he fixed his sink. She hadn't known that the man knew how plumbing stuff worked, but when his sink started to back up, he'd grabbed a toolbox and had gotten to work.

She'd be lying if she didn't admit that she liked seeing him be so capable. Especially since it was with something that she wasn't very skilled at. Back at home, plumbing issues were almost always handled by Charity, Papa and Charlie, which was fine with her.

"What's that?"

"I just want you to know, whatever your answer, I'm chill with it and I won't take offense."

At that he slid himself out from under the sink. Gloveless, hatless, and in just a blue tank and jeans, he looked quite handsome. She could see those delicate, lightning-like scars all across his shoulders and arms, with a streak of schmutz down one of his cheeks.

"That's kinda ominous, Clara."

"Hold on, you have something on your face."

So, sue her, she was stalling. But she felt almost as nervous as she had on her date. And was it a sin to want a little time to bolster herself?

Jumping off the counter, she went to the bathroom and wetted a washcloth. Nathan used to not have a washcloth at all, just a bar of soap, but since she'd been helping him, she'd been slowly integrating more useful things for him. She wasn't one hundred percent certain he was using them, but she'd found them in the wash a couple of times, so that had certainly given her hope.

Coming back, she crouched where Nate was sitting on the floor, a curious expression on his face. He knew something was up, but at least he was polite enough not to ask.

Slowly, Clara dabbed at the spot on his cheek, gently buffing it out. And her tactic definitely worked as a distraction, at least to herself, because once it was gone, her fingers were gently tracing over his skin that had been hidden by the grit.

Was she even breathing? She didn't know. The only thing she was aware of was the feel of him under her fingertips. Smooth, rugged, jagged and curved, it was a conflicting sensory experience, but she liked it.

She wanted to touch more, to trace her fingers down his neck, to map out every scar along his shoulders and down his arms until she had them memorized.

She was so lost in what she was doing, she didn't even realize how long she was caressing him until he caught her hand and pressed his cheek against her palm.

"It doesn't gross you out?"

"Huh?"

"The scars?"

His eyes were avoiding her, and she knew that look. He was slipping into that self-loathing mode of his. Well, that wouldn't do at all.

Leaning forward, she kissed him as softly and tenderly as she knew how. She was crowding him, she knew, practically climbing into his lap, but he certainly didn't complain. No, instead his arms wrapped around her waist, holding onto her as if she was his only lifeline.

When they parted, she cupped his face with both of her

hands, just looking at him, looking at the face of the man that she was growing more and more in love with every single day.

"Your scars are you, and I like *you*. I wish that the accident hadn't happened to you. I wish that you didn't have to go through all that pain, but they're a part of your story. How could I ever think they're gross?"

He didn't say anything, just staring right back up at her. It was perhaps the longest steady eye contact they'd ever had, and Clara willed for him to believe her.

Nathan ended up not saying anything at all, instead kissing her again. Except his kiss wasn't gentle like hers had been, not soothing. No, it was full of heat and desire. It was desperation and joy and so much all at once. Clara could feel her entire body heating up and her heart thundering in her chest.

Time lost its meaning again, rushing past her fingers in a slippery deluge. It was just her and Nathan, melting together—

Gasping, Clara pulled her mouth away. Goodness, Cass hadn't been kidding when she'd said it was easy to get pulled under by desire. Clara had never experienced something like that before.

"I have to ask you something," she blurted, not trusting herself not to kiss Nathan all over again.

He blinked at her, clearly trying to catch up from the sudden swerve in topic. "Right. I, uh, recall you saying something along those lines." He cleared his throat and pulled himself out from under her, helping her to her own feet once he was standing. Clara knew it was time to be serious, but it was hard to with some of her lipstick smeared across his lower lips.

"Oh, um, here. Maybe you want to clean that off a little."

"Clean what off?"

She pointed to his face, and he pulled his phone from a pocket, turning the camera on himself. "Clara Miller, were you trying to give me a subtle makeover?" he accused, taking the cloth from her.

"As much as I think everyone looks better with a bold lip, no, that was not my intention, believe it or not."

"I guess I'll just have to believe you on that one." He finished cleaning his face and then gave her a more serious look. "Alright, no more stalling. What's this ominous question you have to ask me?"

"I, uh, well, I wanted to invite you to dinner. At my house. With my family." His eyes went wide and Clara rushed to get the rest of the info out. "It's just my immediate family! Papa, Charity, Cass and Charlie. Cici isn't on winter break yet and no significant others. I know that social situations are still kind of overwhelming for you, but it'd mean a—"

"I'll do it."

Now it was Clara's turn to blink at him. "You'll do it?"

"Yes."

"And you're sure?"

"I'm sure."

Clara swallowed hard, a bit lost. She'd expected to need to do a little more explaining and a touch more begging. "I... I thought this was going to be a lot harder."

Nathan reached out, taking her hands in his. "Clara, with everything you've done for me, how could I possibly begrudge you a single meal. Besides, I do intend to ask your father for his approval and all that."

"Really? Didn't think you were the type."

"I'm not, generally, but your family is a bit old-fashioned, so I figured I should."

Clara pulled him into a brief hug. "I can't believe you're being so chill about dinner with my family."

And of course, Nathan hugged her back, his strong arms

comforting and secure. "Clara, there's a whole list of incredibly painful things I would do for you without asking a single question. Eating dinner with your family is hardly a trial."

Grinning, Clara kissed him again, a short little peck so she couldn't get distracted. "You're the best, you know that?"

"No, you're definitely the best. I'm just happy to be here to experience it."

"Cheesy," she accused before kissing him one more time.

Okay, maybe two more times.

She didn't think that she would ever get tired of kissing his soft lips.

29

Nathan

*L*ife was good.

Every morning when he woke up, he couldn't believe that he was dating someone as brilliant as Clara. And every time she showed up to help him on the homestead, he couldn't help but feel a little more blessed.

And that feeling of blessing helped chip away at the darkness inside of him. Bit by bit, the bitterness ebbed, and the rage cooled. He kept taking his walks around the church, closer and closer. He kept seeing his therapist, and he kept trying to be better.

Sometimes he stumbled. Sometimes he snapped at Clara or was exceptionally short with her. But she would just have to give him a look, and he would remove himself from the situation until he could apologize. It worked out, even if he felt like an absolute cad every time it happened.

But what was important was that it happened less and less. Even as fall passed and winter started. Winter was hard on him, of course, with the cold and dry air wreaking havoc on his skin and his joints.

"Hey, I got you that lotion the store was out of," Clara said, striding into his kitchen where he was grilling them some cheese sandwiches for their lunch.

"How did you get your hands on that?"

"I had it shipped overnight."

She was still too kind. Incredible. Every day she impressed him even more, and he didn't even think that was possible. "You didn't have to do that."

"I know, but you've been having some trouble. It's better to practice preventative medicine, rather than reactionary medicine."

"When you're right, you're right," he said with a grin. "But don't think I won't get you back."

"I look forward to seeing you try. I like rare seeds and collectibles, thank you very much."

He chuckled, shaking his head as he finished up his food. Trust Clara to ask for garden-related things. One of the things he loved about her.

Oh.

He'd never actually used that word before, not even in his head. He'd always been too scared. But after a little over a month of dating, he was more certain than ever that was exactly what he felt.

Slapping their sandwiches on some small plates, he headed towards his living room. He had intended on having a quick, standing lunch in his kitchen, but he was feeling much lower energy than he had before.

"Hey, are you alright?" Clara asked as he rounded the corner. "You look a little pale?"

"Naw, that's just what winter does to me."

"Are you sure?" her tone was skeptical, but she was always a worrier.

He didn't mind, however, because it meant that someone was looking out for him. It was nice. Everything about Clara was nice.

"Yeah, absolutely."

They sat down and ate their sandwiches, but Nathan only got about halfway through before his stomach twisted with a bit of nausea. "You know, I think I'm gonna go lay down."

"Oh, are you not feeling well?"

"No, it's nothing like that. Just a little wiped out."

"Alright, thank you for listening to your body and resting."

He shot her a crooked grin at that. "Thank you for making that almost not sound like a lecture on self-care."

"I do my best."

Chuckling, he stood and headed towards the stairs.

"Oh, and Nathan?"

"Hmmm?" He turned back to her just in time to catch the lotion that she'd tossed towards his face. "Right. Thanks."

"Of course. I'll take care of things while you rest."

With a nod, he went up the stairs. When he finally slid into bed, his exhaustion well and truly hit him, and he fell deep into slumber.

"NATHAN. Nathan? I need you to wake up. Okay, Nathan?"

Blinking the crust from his eyes, Nathan slowly opened them to see Clara's concerned face hovering over his own.

"Oh good, Nathan! Can you drink this water for me?"

She held up an impossibly cold glass to his lips and he sipped at it. It felt like magic across his lips and mouth. How long had he been asleep?

"You're running a fever, Nathan. I came up here to check on you when you were out for more than six hours. You're burning up. I'm going to call Alejandro while you drink this, okay?"

With a shaking hand, he gripped the glass and continued to sip from it while Clara made the call. He hated that he was making her worried. He really did. She already did so much. Why did his body have to fail her too?

"Hi, yes? Alejandro? It's about Nathan..."

He tried to listen—he needed to be responsible about his own health after all—but once more he slipped back into a deep slumber.

"MR. WESTBROOK? Your vitals are picking up. Can you hear me?"

Nathan blinked back into reality to see someone entirely different above his face. Where was Clara? Where was *he?*

"You're in the hospital, Mr. Westbrook. You were brought here by ambulance about two hours ago. You have a skin infection in one of your largest grafts that is making you very sick."

"Where's Clara?"

"I'm here!" There was a noise of a chair moving and then there she was, at his bedside. Somehow, she looked even more beautiful than usual. "How are you feeling, sweetheart? I drove right behind the ambulance the entire way here. You really scared me."

"I'm sorry..."

"No, no, you don't have to apologize. I'm just glad we got you in."

"Yes, time is of the essence," the doctor confirmed. "But I'm afraid this graft is not salvageable without risking it going into your bloodstream or causing other issues."

That was bad. Sure, Nathan wasn't all there, but he was there enough to know that that was bad. "So, what then?"

"It means we need to remove it and get you a new one. Normally I would suggest using your skin by slowly stretching with a subdermal balloon, but I'm concerned such stress could damage other grafts you have.

"My recommendation is that we look for people who would be willing to do the subdermal balloon procedure for you, then allow us to harvest their skin. It's a lengthy process, requiring multiple weeks of expansion then multiple weeks of recovery.

"I'll do it!" Clara said almost before the doctor finished.

"And I'll do it too. I'm game."

Wait, who was that? Craning his neck, Nathan realized that Charlie and Papa Miller were both in the room, sitting quietly in the corner.

"No, neither of you have to do that." Nathan didn't know why he refused, but it was a knee-jerk reaction. He was so tired of being a burden to people, he didn't want to ask even more from the Millers. Talk about the skin off their backs.

"What kind of partner would I be if I didn't help my boyfriend? Let me do this for you."

Nathan pressed his lips together. He knew that tone when Clara got it, and it was her determined to do anything tone. There was no stopping her now.

"I..."

"And I'm sorry, Mr. Westbrook. I know this is not good news, but because of the severity of your condition, we're going to need to get you into surgery tonight. You'll most likely be in the hospital for a week, maybe two. We understand that's not ideal, but considering your compromised immune system, we want to be as careful as possible."

"Two weeks?" Clara practically shouted. Even Nathan knew that was a bit loud in his own ears. "But I didn't even get to invite him to Christmas dinner!"

Now Nathan definitely caught that. "You were going to invite me to Christmas dinner with your family?"

"Of course! What kind of Christmas would it be without you there? Don't you want to spend the holidays with me?"

He nodded, his throat feeling thick. Was it silly to be emotional over a single meal? Probably, but he was feverish and some of his skin was literally killing him, so he felt like he was entitled.

"I did. I mean, I do. I would like that very much."

"You just worry about healing," Papa Miller said, standing up. "We'll take care of the rest."

That seemed to solve it, and the doctor started talking more, but then Nathan's brain caught on something that suddenly seemed very, very important.

"Wait, did you call me your boyfriend?" he asked, looking to Clara with wide eyes.

She looked at him like he was crazy, but what did she expect? "Yes, why?"

"So is that my official title now?"

"Mr. Westbrook, we need you to sign some consent paperwork."

"If you don't mind, I need just a few more minutes please. I'm having a very important conversation." While he was covered in sweat and his brain felt like it'd been flattened with a meat tenderizer.

"Why are you asking that? Was there any doubt that you were my boyfriend? Do you not want to be my boyfriend?"

There was that worry in her tone. The one he never got because he would be absolutely insane to ever leave her. If their relationship ever ended, it would be because Clara woke up and realized he was so far below her league he needed a ladder to get up to her.

"Well, I knew we were dating, but I thought I, you know... I had to be better. Make myself worthy of you."

"Oh, *Nathan*. You don't have to work yourself to some impossible standard to be my boyfriend. That was never our agreement. You're worthy of me right here and now. The only thing I've ever asked of you is to keep working on yourself, and you've done exactly that."

"...oh."

Well, he had certainly made things much more complicated than they needed to be.

"Mr. Westbrook, we really need to get that consent signed for your surgery. The doctor is waiting on you."

"Nurse, if you don't mind giving me just one more little moment. I just want to give my girlfriend a kiss before I go in."

"Don't worry, Nathan. I'll be here until you get out of surgery. We all will."

"I know. Now how about that kiss?"

With the tiniest of laughs, she bent down and pressed a kiss to his lips. Hers felt so refreshingly cool against his that he wanted to stay that way forever. But apparently it went on for too long, because both the nurse and Papa Miller cleared their throat.

"Sorry," Clara said a bit breathlessly.

Hey, feverish and half dying, but he still had it. That wasn't half bad.

"I'll see you after surgery, Nathan."

"I'll see you soon."

NATHAN LOOKED out the window at the gray day that had turned into a very gray night. The hospital was all decorated and he could hear carols playing gently in the halls outside, but he wasn't entirely concerned. The holidays had never really been his thing, and they were even less of his thing when he was stuck in the hospital.

But he couldn't be entirely ungrateful. His skin graft had been removed without any complications, and the infection was completely cleared up after a week on some pretty serious antibiotics. It would have been nice to go home, but considering the strain the antibiotics put on his guts and the fact that he had a whole patch of skin missing, the doctors didn't want to risk him becoming reinfected.

There were other upsides as well, he couldn't deny. Clara and Charlie were both going through the uncomfortable subdermal expansions, and she'd been texting him pictures from their Christmas celebration all day long.

Apparently, it was a big to-do because Mick was there, celebrating his first Christmas with Cass. According to Clara, the tall cowboy had gotten the second eldest sister the perfect presents and the entire family was weepy about it.

It wasn't as good as being there himself, but it was nicer than being completely excluded. The worst part was, however, that since he'd been so sick, he hadn't been able to go home and wrap Clara's present.

He'd ordered it all the way back before Thanksgiving, when they'd decided to have their own mini-dinner together the day after Clara's celebration with her family. She'd floated the idea of him coming to her place for a moment, but both of them agreed that it wasn't quite the right time. He was doing better in social situations, but considering that some of her cousins were coming from up north and from Texas, plus Alejandro and his little daughter, that was too overwhelming for him.

It frustrated him to think it was probably just sitting in his mail pile in a cardboard box, but once he was out of the hospital, he'd be able to give it to her and see the look on her face.

But only after he wrapped it. And put it in another box. And then another bigger box. He'd watched enough old movies with both his grandmother and Clara to understand sometimes the dramatics of the present were just as important as the contents.

His phone buzzed again, and he looked down to see it was Clara texting that she was on her way. He grinned at his phone, his mood already lifting. Maybe he was even more of a sap than he was before, but every day he fell in love with her a little more.

Boyfriend, huh? He couldn't believe he hadn't picked that up. It was so obvious in retrospect, but they'd never actually used the words. Where was the line between casually dating, dating, and being boyfriend and girlfriend?

Behind him, apparently. And he couldn't be happier for it.

It was hard not to be antsy as he waited for Clara to arrive, but eventually she did, two large bags hanging from her arms. Nathan sat up in his bed, excitement running through him.

"Who would have thought, I got exactly what I wanted for Christmas."

"What? You haven't even opened them yet."

"I wasn't talking about anything in the bags."

"Geez, you're cheesy for a sick guy." She rolled her eyes like she always did when he was especially cheesy. But she liked it, despite her protestations.

"That's because I'm not really sick anymore. Just a bit patchy."

"Hah, that's one way to put it. But once this balloon in my thigh is as big as it's supposed to be, you won't be patchy anymore."

"How is that going, by the way?"

He looked her over with concern. She was wearing another one of her fancy dresses, and it was clear that it was one that she'd made specifically for Christmas, considering the green velvet and red piping with white fur trim.

Funny, before he'd started dating Clara, he'd definitely had no idea what 'piping' was beyond the plumbing term. But since they'd been together, he'd learned about that, princess seams, bias tape—which wasn't tape at all—and what 'straight sizes' were as opposed to 'plus sizes.' Fashion was incredibly complicated, and it just affirmed his opinions that he didn't need much outside of flannels, jeans and sweatpants.

"Not bad! It's a little uncomfy, but as long as I remember to lotion it and stay plenty hydrated, I can usually forget it's there for a while. I've learned not to wear heels though. I don't know why, but it definitely makes it feel a little weird."

"But no pain?"

"No, no pain, Nathan."

He narrowed his eyes at her, and while that look usually ruffled some people, Clara just smiled blithely at him. "And you'd tell me if you were in pain, right?"

"You know I would. I would never lie to you."

That was very true. Clara was many things, but a liar was nowhere on that list. "You're right. You're right. So what did you bring me?"

"Well, let me bring that table over and I'll set everything up."

"Set everything up? Sounds fancy."

"Oh yes, super fancy. I crammed a whole orchestra in here, you know."

"Considering it's you, I wouldn't doubt it."

"Why, because I'm over the top?"

"No, but if anyone had the powers of Mary Poppins and her bottomless bag, it'd be you."

She blushed and waved him off, as she always did when he surprised her with a compliment. He loved seeing that color flood her cheeks just as much as he had before, but it meant even more with every passing day. Especially when it was paired with her bashful smile that she tried to hide as she busied herself.

"You're silly."

"You're the only one that thinks so."

Their banter continued as she set up, and Nathan didn't know why he was surprised when he saw her empty one bag of nearly a dozen packages. He hadn't asked for anything for Christmas. She was already giving him a chunk of her skin. That seemed like plenty of gifts and then some.

"I don't have anything for you," he muttered when she turned to him, shame creeping up his neck. He'd gotten a whole lot better at his feelings of inadequacy, but every now and then they reared their head again. "What I ordered came in the mail while I was in here."

"Oh, that's fine. Besides, these are more for the both of us, considering how often I'm at your place working on things."

He chuckled at that. "You could be over more if you wanted."

"Nathan, if I was over anymore, I'd be living there."

"I know."

That stopped her right where she was and she stared at him. "Nathan..."

He held up his hands, sensing the tension suddenly expanding in her chest. "Sorry, I know it's too soon. I was just saying... I'm serious. When I think about my future, you're in it. Every single day, the two of us, working side by side together."

The shocked look faded, replaced by one of genuine affection that he couldn't believe he was lucky enough to see. "Thank you, Nathan. It means a lot to hear that."

"Well then, I'll say it as many times as you'd like to hear."

Table forgotten, she flounced over to him and pressed a kiss to his lips. Goodness, he could kiss her forever and that still wouldn't feel like enough for him.

"Merry Christmas, my love," Clara said.

Love?

Sure, Nathan had long since learned that he loved her, but he hadn't said it out loud. Mostly because he was waiting to feel like he was good enough. But hadn't Clara said he was already worthy? He always said he respected her enough to trust her, so what choice did he have but to believe her.

And by that logic, if she said she loved him...

"Love, huh?"

"Yes," Clara whispered, looking at him with bright, shining eyes. "Is that okay?"

"It's more than okay. Because I love you, Clara, more than anything. And I'm sorry that I wasn't brave enough to admit that before you said it."

"It's alright, Nathan, because I've known for weeks."

"You have?"

Her hand caressed his chest, and he was sure that she could feel his heart thundering there. "Of course."

"How?"

"How could I not? It's in everything you do. It's in the way you hold my hand when we go for walks with the fireflies. It's in the way you let me name one of your newest chickens. It's in the way you look at me while I'm cooking and you think I don't see. It's in how you cook for me even though you're self-conscious about what you make."

Nathan didn't know what to say about that. He could only stare at her, mouth mildly agape. She... she saw all that?

"You learned sewing terms for me just because you know that I love making myself nice things. You learned the difference between a sewing machine and a serger, just so you could have better conversations with me. You don't tease me for anything that I love, whether it's gardening, makeup or animals. And, I'm sorry, but Charity let it slip that you asked her what cruelty-free was since you remembered me mentioning it once."

She was looking at him like he was the entire world, and wow. Just wow. He'd never known that he had been waiting his whole life to be looked at like that, but suddenly, he knew without a doubt that her expression was what had always been missing for him.

Being looked at like *that,* like he mattered, like he mattered so intensely to her that she wanted him in her life forever, was more than he could ever ask for. And yet she kept looking at him, strong, beautiful, kind Clara.

"You see, Nate, you've been loving me for a long time now, and maybe you weren't at the point where you could say it, but everything you did said it for you. And I want you to know, I love you just as fiercely. I love you, Nathan Westbrook, and I want to spend the rest of my life with you."

"And I want to spend it with you," Nathan murmured before

kissing her again. He kissed her and kissed her, trying to put all of his feelings into it. When they parted, her lips were swollen and her face was flushed, making her that much more beautiful. "You know, none of those presents you brought are going to be that impressive considering you just gave me the best Christmas present I could ever ask for."

"Well, in that case, Merry Christmas."

"Merry Christmas indeed."

EPILOGUE: NATHAN

"Are you ready?"

Nathan nodded, looking out of the Jeep's window to see his house. He wasn't sure what he expected, maybe cobwebs or it to look half dilapidated in his month-long absence, but surprisingly it was spick-and-span. He should have known better, of course. Clara would never let it degrade after she'd put so much work into it.

"More ready than you know," he said, letting all the breath he hadn't known he'd been holding rush out of him. "It's been a long haul, hasn't it?"

"Goodness, yes. But what's important is that you're out of the hospital and have your doctor's seal of approval. Gold star and everything."

"Yes, I behaved and got my good boy sticker," Nathan said with a huff. Which was really a record for him. Normally he was a much more... combative patient. A real type A, as Alejandro called him. But he made sure to never push himself and followed his doctor's advice to the letter, mostly so he wouldn't disappoint Clara.

Because finally, he had some hope to get better *for*. When he'd laid in the hospital right after his accident, he'd felt like there was no reason to live, nothing worth fighting for or achieving.

"You did. And because you were so good, I didn't organize a surprise party for you and instead went with your favorite meal."

"BBQ ribs with Spanish rice n' beans plus cornbread?"

"Exactly that."

"What are we waiting for then?"

She grinned impishly at him. He loved it whenever she got that mischievous look. Actually, he just loved being around her in general.

"My sentiments exactly."

Finally getting out of her car, he walked right up to his front door. Truth was, he was feeling much stronger and steady than he had in months. He hadn't been aware that he'd had an infection slowly growing in him, taking root and making him burn with a steadily rising fever, and being completely healed from that was a gift. Plus, having another two weeks after his graft to let it heal without pushing himself had certainly helped.

And maybe that vitality was what encouraged him to ask something he never would have otherwise.

"Could I carry you over the threshold?"

"What?"

"I, uh, I would like to carry you over."

"What, like we're married?"

The shocked expression on her face definitely made him nervous, but he pressed on. "No. More like a promise."

"A promise?"

"Yeah, for the future. When I built this place, I was utterly alone and thought that was right for me. But now I know better. I'm a better person because you're here. And I don't think I'm meant to be alone anymore."

"In that case..." There was the red color across her cheeks, and he bent down to kiss each one in turn. "Won't that be bad for your graft?"

"It'll be for less than a minute, and the doctor cleared me for general homesteading work as long as I listen to my body. And right now, my body, as well as my heart, is telling me that I really, really want you to be in my future."

"Well... alright then. Let's give it a try."

He knew he was grinning madly, but he didn't care. Bending at the knee, he swept Clara up in a bridal carry. It wasn't exactly easy, considering she was six feet tall and muscled enough to complete any chore needed on a ranch, but he managed. There was once a time where he might have been able to throw her around, but it would still take a lot more physical therapy to get back to that point.

But once she was in his arms, he once more was struck by just how *right* it felt, and with a nudge of his foot to the door, he was carrying her over the threshold.

"You know, my Papa would be pretty infuriated to know that we did that."

"Would he?" Nathan asked, gently putting her onto the ground. "Well, I guess we better not tell him."

"I won't if you don't," she murmured before pushing herself up on her tiptoes and pressing her lips to his.

Just like always, he felt like he could kiss her until he ran out of air, water and everything else a human might need. But they did eventually have to part, and when they did, he suddenly realized that his whole house smelled *amazing*.

"You said something about my favorite meal?"

"I did indeed." She slipped her hand in his and tugged him towards the kitchen. "Come on, let's go eat. Together."

Together. That sounded exactly right. Because together is exactly how he wanted to spend the rest of his life.

EPILOGUE: CLARA

Thunder boomed ahead, so loud that it rattled the very foundation of Nathan's cabin. It was intensely powerful, enough to make even Clara jump where she was lighting candles in the kitchen.

Goodness, the fall season was the absolute worst for lightning storms. Did they have to be so vicious? It was like the sky and the ground were complaining about the heat of summer by throwing a bunch of temper tantrums when it cooled down in the fall.

At least Nathan was in a much better spot than he'd been the year before. With a little over nine months of therapy, both physical and mental, he was doing much, much better. Of course there were always setbacks, or bad days, but on the whole, he was nearly back to full health.

He was always going to have dizzy spells, they were pretty sure, and a hypersensitivity to temperature changes with his skin. Not to mention an increased susceptibility to dangerous sunburns, but it wasn't all bad. He'd gained weight, his clothes were no longer hanging from him, and his stamina had much increased. He no longer needed a stool to wash his dishes or cook. He didn't need a special stool for the garden or his shower. It was wonderful, really, seeing him flourish with every single passing day.

She couldn't believe that it'd only been about a year since they met officially. To her, it felt like he'd always been in her life. He was a constant form of reassurance for her and, finally, she was beginning to believe what he and her family said about her.

Maybe with a wee pinch of salt, though.

Another truly ear-splitting boom and Clara almost screamed again. And she *liked* thunderstorms. It was just the booms were coming so quick and close together without any warning that it was hard not to shriek.

She should probably go check on Nathan.

Trying to project an air of cool, she headed to the living room where she'd left him with the dinner she'd just finished cooking. But to her surprise, he looked relatively fine. Slightly agitated, yeah, but fine.

"Nathan?"

He jolted a little, his head whipping towards her, and then a big, cheery smile spread across his features. "Hey there, gorgeous. You okay?"

"I'm okay. Are you?"

"I think I'm alright."

Carefully, Clara set the candles she had brought onto a couple of secure surfaces and gave him a good look over. There was a touch of sweat on his brow, a flush to his cheeks, and his right foot was bouncing. Reaching into her nearly encyclopedic knowledge of Nathan and all his various ticks, she tried to piece that all together.

Hmmm, something was definitely up. He was agitated for sure, but not afraid. And he very clearly was entirely himself.

...interesting.

"Not that I'm not grateful, but you seem to be taking this storm pretty well."

"It is a doozy, isn't it?"

There was something about his tone as well. Something strange. She couldn't put her finger quite on it though, and that made her even more curious.

"It is."

She sat down beside him and tried to pretend that everything was alright, but the mystery of it was bugging her. She liked to think that she knew Nathan like the back of her hand, but how he was acting was throwing her for a loop.

She made it about two minutes before something bubbled up. "Is everything okay?"

"Yeah, why wouldn't it be?"

"Well... it's just... there's a big storm out there and normally these situations are, uh, are... a little more fraught."

"I guess I just have something much more important on my mind."

"More important?"

"Yeah. Exactly that."

She wanted to pester more, but she also didn't want to push it. "Okay. Do you want to watch a movie then?"

"Yeah. How about the *King and I*?"

"Oh, yes! Good choice!" Clara jumped up to get it and soon she was able to forget about Nathan's strange behavior.

Well... almost forget.

He kept fiddling with his phone during the entire climax of the movie, the most beautiful part that made her cry. It was a bit irritating, but she tried not to say anything. Or at least she did until it got to the big finale. By then, it was just too much, and she paused it.

"Huh? What happened?"

"I just... is there something distracting you? You've been on your phone for ages."

"Have I?" he murmured.

"Nathan, you—"

Clara cut herself off as music started to fill the room. It was a familiar song, but one she hadn't heard in about a year. It took her a moment, but she realized it was coming from the portable Bluetooth speaker she'd gotten Nathan for Christmas.

It was the slow dance song from *Some Like it Hot.*

"Nathan... what's going on?" she murmured, eyes wide. But when she looked back to where he'd been sitting, Nathan was no longer there.

No, he was kneeling on the ground in front of her, holding a small open box in his hand.

"Nathan?"

"Clara Miller, you've changed my life more than I could ever say. I fully believe that without you, I would be dead. Every day with you is better than the last, and I feel myself becoming more and more of the type of man who could possibly deserve you.

"I love you. I love you so much that it hurts, but I want it to keep hurting because it's the best feeling I've ever had.

"Now, I know I don't have a lot to my name, and I know that you deserve everything good in the world and more, but gosh if I don't want to spend the rest of my life trying to give you just that. The moon, the stars, and especially a large garden, whatever it is that makes you smile. And I want to be there to see that smile. I want to build a life with you, because I know that whatever that life is, it's the best one I could possibly ever have."

Oh *goodness.*

Clara was crying. Hot, ugly, giant tears down her cheeks. She hated crying because it always made her nose run and her eyes blaze red along with a headache rolling in soon after, but she didn't care.

"Nathan Westbrook, you better not be joking right now because I will literally throw you into your own pigpen," she warbled, her voice cracking.

"I'm not joking, Clara," he answered, and at least his voice sounded thick too. "Miss Clara Miller, would you do me the honor of marrying me?"

"I do! I mean, I will! Yes, Nathan! YES!"

She was squealing, loud and bright, but she didn't care about that either. Clapping, she reached out to him, and he slid the ring right onto her finger.

It was a beautiful thing, a bright, shimmering gold with her birthstone right at its center. "You remembered I don't like diamonds."

"I did," he said, rising up with her hands in his. "I love you. And I love learning everything about you."

"I'm so happy! And so excited!" Clara said.

"I feel..." He paused for a moment, and that look he gave her just grew thicker between them. "Lucky. And very, very much in love."

"If you're so in love, then kiss me," she murmured, swept up in everything he'd said. Despite her runny nose and teary eyes, he kissed her, and not for the first time, Clara felt like she could float away from the earth with the beauty of it. There was so much in his kisses. They were an oath, a promise, full of desire and want and everything she'd always thought was never supposed to be hers.

But when she was with Nathan, she truly believed that she

was the leading lady, that she deserved every bit of his affection and spotlight. She couldn't imagine ever giving that up.

And now, she wouldn't have to. It was her and Nathan, for the rest of their lives. Working together to be better, stronger and more loving.

And she couldn't wait.

Did you enjoy reading about Clara and Nathan? Ready to read about the other two Miller families? *Brothers of Miller Ranch* is about the Miller family in Montana and *Miller Brothers of Texas* is about the Miller family in, you guessed it, Texas.

If you haven't already, I hope you decide to go on the rest of the Miller family journey with me!

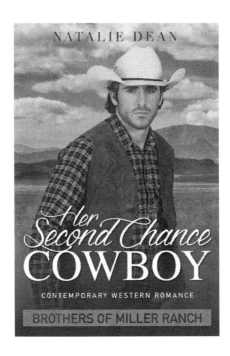

Brothers of Miller Ranch Book One

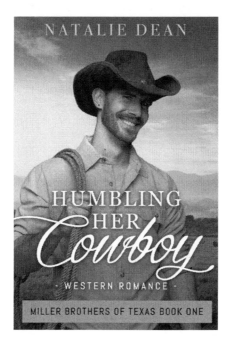

Miller Brothers of Texas Book One

EXCLUSIVE BOOKS BY NATALIE DEAN

GET THREE FREE BOOKS when you join my Sweet Romance Newsletter :)

Get One Free Contemporary Western Romance:
The New Cowboy at Miller Ranch, Miller Brothers of Texas Prologue - He's a rich Texas rancher. She's just a tomboy ranch employee. Can she make him see life can still be happy without all that money?

AND Two Free Historical Western Romances:
Spring Rose - A feel good historical western mail-order groom novelette about a broken widow finding love and faith.

Fools Rush In - A historical western mail-order bride novelette based off a true story!

Go to nataliedeanauthor.com to find out how to join!

ABOUT AUTHOR - NATALIE DEAN

Born and raised in a small coastal town in the south I realized at a young age that I was more adventurous than my conservative friends and family. I loved to travel. My passion for travel opened up a whole new world and new cultures to me that I will always be grateful for.

I was raised to treasure family. I always knew that at some point in my life I would leave my storybook life behind and become someone's mother, someone's aunt and hopefully someone's grandmother. Little did I know that the birth of my son later in life would make me the happiest I've ever been. He will always be my biggest achievement. The strong desire to be a work-from-home mom is what lead me down this path of publishing books.

While I have always loved reading I never realized how much I would love writing until I started. I feel like each one of my books have been influenced by someone or something I've experienced in my life. To be able to share this gift has become a dream come true.

I hope you enjoy reading them as much as I have enjoyed creating them. I truly hope to develop an ongoing relationship with all of my readers that lasts into my last days :)

www.nataliedeanauthor.com

Made in the USA
Monee, IL
12 April 2021

65558807R00143